AS THE SUN SMILES

C. L. HODGE

As the Sun Smiles

Editor: E. Lee Caleca and Ms. Cheri Boring
Proofreader: Dr. Robin E. Campbell
Text Format: Maureen Cutajar
Cover Art: Ben Kerschaw
Cover Format: Caligraphics http://caligraphics.net/
Chapter images courtesy of Shutterstock.com/AF Studio contributor

Summary: Growing up in a non-traditional, nuclear family, Alex long claimed the responsibility of raising younger brother Willie. At the beginning of America's worst fear, this same self-proclaimed responsibility is challenged to the brink of failure. When it matters most, Alex soon finds out if striving for this responsibility was ever possible or for naught.

ISBN 978-0-692-78635-2 [1. Strength-Fiction 2. Responsibility-Fiction 3. American Fear-Fiction 4. Family-Fiction 5. Resilience-Fiction 6. Terrorism]

ISBN-13: 978-0-692-78635-2
ISBN-10: 069278635X

Printed in America

For any further questions or requests,
contact Corey "Legend" Hodge at:
C.L.Hodge92@gmail.com

This book is:

An Achievement dedicated to my resting mother
Arvene Darlene Hodge-Hawes;

An Achievement that couldn't have been done without
the continuous support of loved ones;

An Achievement, a product I hope will inspire the young minds
of those from East Knoxville as well as the many communities
similar to it throughout Knoxville, Tennessee,
the United States, and even the world.

The success of this book will not be determined by the number of
copies it sells. It can sell copies by the millions—which would be
awesome—but if it doesn't inspire someone to take a similar
chance of releasing their creativity, this book is a failure.
—Corey "Legend" Hodge

1

AFTER:

"Tell me, Alex."

"Okay."

2

DURING:

"You'd think it was a stormy day; that or one of those excessively melancholic days. One of those days where stretched out clouds were in a mobile stagnation. It wasn't one of those days or anything close to one; no, it was the complete opposite. That day, that evening wasn't beautiful, it *was* beauty; kind of how she always was. Around us, below, under, and behind us, it was a day that the senses worked collectively to define to us the beauty of nature. The chill carried along the winds *felt* pushing against my face; the *hearing* of the grand orchestra of leaves whispering, birds of many types all humming, all accompanied by the white noise often and easily neglected; *smell* and *taste* accented one another. The scent of honeysuckles inhabited my nose to the extent that I could taste the secret of their sweetness. Sight though, the most impactful of all—just as long as I looked up. Regardless of what was happening, regardless of how sick I became, regardless of the horrors that unpredictably and confidently knocked at our front door, the overshadowing of the terrors of masks, or the shock felt from still trying to comprehend the loss of our loved ones, what allowed sight to still remain beautiful was noticing, there above us, the inviting smile of the Sun.

The sky was of a utopia; possibly *the* most ironic thing I remembered to blitz across my brain. It was crazy how in a matter of time, life drastically contradicted the utopia that senses strived to create for me and Willie. But even the utopia seen and felt was easily and always erased without a trace as soon as they could be seen and heard marching down Milligan.

Regardless, the sun still remained smiling.

3

THE YEAR BEFORE:

"At different points in history, it seemed as though mass murders had become frequent, class. Less than a week after one, people were already being told of another; and yet just days after one, people are already back to focusing on their favorite sports team or phone application—"

"All you have to say is 'app' Mr. Hodge," a student on his phone carelessly interrupted.

"You see!" He began with even more passion than he had already started with. "What is, where is the remorse? Does fear pertaining to a possible tomorrow exist anymore? Where is the desire to change, to fix what is obviously broken? People don't care until it's at their front door. Have you heard of those terrorists? They claim to be abou-"

It was one of those days. Mr. Hodge came to class reading some article and from there, he was on his soapbox.

"Alex, what is sympathy?" he asked, snapping me out of my usual daydream.

I didn't know why he asked me. "It's, it's- sympathy is like wh—"
Bell rings
"Sorry, sir."

Before walking completely out of class, I could see out the corner of my eye Mr. Hodge standing behind his desk. There showing his level of disappointment in me, in the class, was nothing rare. Everything down to his posture was of a cycle. Every time, disappointment was exemplified by the hanging of his head below shoulders; his entire body supported by his two hands clutched to the opposing sides of his desk; as his head hung, it swung in brief shifts from side to side in an almost rhythmic fashion. My head flung completely away from him when I saw that he looked to me.

Mr. Hodge was a man around the same age as Mom—just over 40ish. There was always something about him able to be felt from the first time I met him—though our first impressions were horrible. He always told us, almost as if it came with an award, that he had been teaching for close to a decade at East High School. For almost a decade, he remained at a school that had the reputation of Hell within it.

Though I had already met him, it was my sophomore year that I was in his class.

"My name is Mr. Hodge," I remember him introducing himself to us during our first class with him. "Not only am I your English teacher, I am also the social instructor that I feel many of you need."

"That is not included anywhere in the syllabus," a star athlete jokingly said almost immediately after Mr. Hodge said this. He received a few responsive chuckles and smirks, but whimpered back down into his seat as Mr. Hodge gave him a deathly stare.

"It is students like yourself, sir, that bring me here and keep me here. I was once in your seat at this same school many years ago. Many of the problems leaders saw then are the same problems this school and community are dealing with now. One of them being the desire to be the class clown which further shows an extreme lack of respect. I have set out to include, as I teach you the essentials of the curriculum, sort of common sense or vocational skills including the development of respect, sir," Mr. Hodge responded despite knowing that only half of what he said was actually listened to.

As Mr. Hodge went on, more and more students began to zone out—myself included. Still, I could tell that his being here at the school, here of all places, had to mean that he cared. While English was a class I never did well in—always high "C", low "B" grades—I liked Mr. Hodge.

4

JUST BEFORE THE RETURN:

"Alex, there's another one," Mom announced.

"Already? I haven't even finished the other, and you already have another one for me?"

"You said you needed more money. I've always worked for mine when I was your age and still do. Twenty dollars a lawn is easy money in a small neighborhood of wealthy lazies. If I didn't have you and your brother, even at my age I'd be doing these yards by the hour. You just don't appre—"

"Mom, I said I was gonna do it? I was jus—"

"Alex, watch your tone. I'm not in the mood. There was a protest earlier. It was in Macon, Georgia."

"A protest? Have there been any more sightings?"

"So far, no. So far."

"The protests though, they're happening all over the place. Have there been any arrests?" I questioned. Having already answered my first question, I only asked about the protest just to show some sense of a misleading sympathy.

Not catching on to my present carelessness, "Several; there has been lots of public damage as well. It's crazy that this has been what and where we've returned to, as a nation. As much as I wished it didn't, it did, in just under a month or so. It's almost as if nothing *at all* had ever happened. It all started with the death of that celebrity that maybe Ms. Darlene would've known about and then everything was forgotten.

"Dinner is about ready. I'll call and tell the neighbors that something came up and you will do their lawns tomorrow. Go and get your little brother, please."

I crept through the hallway trying to make nothing more than the sound of a single falling leaf landing in the center of a lake, but still wanting to be as a shark makings its rounds, a lion having been patient for a minute. Step. Pause. Step. Pause. Closer and then closer I approached my prey. I felt this drip of sweat waltzing from my eyebrows. Desperately trying to go unnoticed and yet another step brought a certain creak loyal only to wooden floors like ours. Pause. Still, no response.

"Gotcha!" I all but yelled but received no response.

"Alex, shhh. This is the best part," Willie said without even turning from the TV.

"You and those cartoons," I told him, slightly irritated. "Come on, it's dinner time."

After Willie finally turned off the TV and sat at the dinner table in the kitchen, I again remember having a certain thought. For years, I always acknowledged that we were not, did not, and could never fit the image of America's nuclear family. Though not the typical white, middle-class, church going, always smiling, *privileged* family, we still made do.

Before eating, as if to say a prayer, I would always look at the picture of Ms. Darlene that, shortly after her death and as a symbol of the thanks we'd for years owed her, we hung on the wall next to our dinner table. In her remembrance, regardless of the struggle I had, did, or would endure, I vowed to never forget or neglect that we were still blessed.

Close to a month after her passing, "Thank you, Ms. Darlene," was a whisper that became habitually said by me as Willie separately said grace.

"Tell me about your day, Willie. Where did you and Alex volunteer at today?" was the same cliché questions always used to begin our dinner conversations. Nuclear, no, but still a family, yes.

5

We didn't have the "nuclear" family that seemed common in our branch of the urban community and the communities like ours. For comfort, several times I told myself that a "nuclear" family was unquestionably a luxury, but not a necessity. Me and Willie were only a few years apart, but sometimes it felt like decades. I never really knew our dad and mom had 3 jobs to make up for his absence, a death she never talked about. The most I knew of him was that my name was based after him, but that, to me, though it probably should have, meant nothing.

Aside from the two or three jobs Mom always transitioned between, an unofficial job she always had was being something along the lines of a housemaid for Ms. Darlene. Because of this, along with the brittleness I remember Ms. Darlene always having, especially as I got older, I had the unofficial job of raising Willie. At different occasions I remembered times came that I had to teach him, wash him, feed him, and tuck him. There came points that I even had to fight for him and regardless, I always told myself that I would never hesitate to fight for him again; there came a point that I instilled within myself that I was willing to even die for him if such a time came. It was frustrating at times, but with all this being done for him by me that meant there were now a few less things Mom had to worry about as she endlessly strived to provide for us.

Though sometimes we were able to go to church, I *didn't* believe in or feel that I had to belong to a religion to still acknowledge that we were blessed. Extremely blessed. My Mom only being her housemaid, what I was eventually able to comprehend that exceeded "the benefits," of only being a housemaid, ever since I could remember, we always lived *with* Ms. Darlene.

To this very point, she remains the most gorgeous woman I've ever seen and known. She alone showed me that beauty included but was so much more than a physical trait. I always had a theory to how we got to living with Ms. Darlene. I feel like it started with her somehow seeing the financial struggle our family was in. Though Mom never told this to me, I knew that Mom's pride would never allow her to simply live with or what she may have felt was off someone. I think to get around this, Ms. Darlene generously hired mom to be her "housemaid." I imagine that mom was iffy about this, but accepted the offer and from then remained Ms. Darlene's housemaid ever since. Again though, none of this was ever confirmed which left all of this as nothing more than a theory.

We were the family, or at least the loved ones Ms. Darlene always wanted; we gave her a love that she for decades longed for, while she provided the security Mom often told me that we were deprived of.

Some of our peers practically hated me and Willie. While we lived in a rougher part of the city, living with Ms. Darlene, we lived in what Mr. Hodge would call "the gentrified" portion of our city. The streets were neatly paved, cars of neighbors were more expensive, houses were secured not only by security systems, but by stationary cops parked on corners as nights would come and leave. Because we lived with Ms. Darlene, we experienced a number of luxuries that many, just blocks away, had little to no exposure to.

I remember coming home from school one day. While in our neighborhood, I had gotten in a fight with a kid that told Willie that our family were "parasites" living off Ms. Darlene. "The parasites" became our identity to some of the kids within our block. It was a sort of demographic that, though we were rarely called it in person, often we were still covertly called "Parasites."

"What exactly is a parasite?" one boy student once asked in a biology class.

My heart immediately began to beat faster. I looked over at the kid who asked it, but eye contact was declined. All that I saw was a smirk which told me everything I needed to know about the student's question to the teacher.

"We haven't gotten there yet. In a few chapters, I will answer all your questions and tell you all that you need to know about the parasitic kingdom," the teacher responded, completely unaware of the insult being made.

"Can you please just describe them to me? I swear I saw one and still see a couple of them *all* the time."

The class, too, knew that my family was who the boy was referencing with his sloppy questions. Several students began chuckling. Many looked at me out of the corner of their eyes, but as I looked back at them, they would quickly jolt their eyes back towards the teacher; they continued chuckling.

"Well, sir, I like a curious mind," the teacher responded in an ecstatic sense. I felt a combination of fury and embarrassment beginning to surge. My heartbeat continued to bang. The pulse in my head genuinely had me wondering whether or not my head would explode.

"A parasite is a thing, an organism that thrives off of other things."

"Kind of like a *tape or ringworm?*"

"Exactly!" The teacher nearly shouted and then continued, "Some of our goals in the science field, while studying, are to also get rid of the parasites that plague our everyday surroundings."

I left class that day without saying a single word.

Despite the generosity of Ms. Darlene, we still shared many of the struggles that our "fellow" low-income families endured. We had no choice but to sometimes wear the unfashionable tears in our jeans accented with having to always wear the dirt and scuffles on our once white, but still off-brand shoes. Being black, in this high-income portion of the community, we were the isolated geese in a "duck-duck-goose" game. We were of the few— if not the only—in our part of the neighborhood that could find satisfaction from finding a dollar on the ground.

Shortly after summer break had started, starting with a single day, this was when everything began to change.

Coming from the same kid that asked the question in the biology class, "Those parasites," I heard him say loudly while overtly pointing as if introducing us, monuments, to a number of visiting foreigners from another state or even country.

That day, I was easily overcome with embarrassment as me and Willie were now the center of several attentions. Some joined in the pointing towards us. Others looked with severe disgust as if looking at slithering, slimly parasites on the side of a gutter.

"Screw it," I thought, *"Screw him."*

It was as if I forgot that my fists and the boy's face weren't magnetized together. For the first time, I thought: in a sense, if I had done nothing I would've accepted being called a parasite. From every punch landing on the sides of his face, I felt better, as if thriving off of the pain I knew I was causing.

"Stop it!" screeched a voice.

I realized I had blacked-out. It was as if I, the parasite, experienced an overload shutdown.

There on the ground, the boy spat out blood like toothpaste in a sink. From the overload, I came back to reality; as I looked around, it wasn't the fear in the kids' eyes that scared me most though. I could care less about fear breaching the bodies of those who were just pointing to and isolating me and Willie. It was grasp of the fear reaching from Willie that scared, paralyzed me.

Lifting up from the boy who was now shriveled over like a browned, dried-out flower in a desert, I turned to Willie and mandated, "Let's go." I almost stuttered when I said this. I demanded this to him, but Willie didn't move. He stood there looking as if he were still processing everything that just happened. Again I yelled "Let's go," but this time grabbing his hand, trucking through the others, I pulled him through streets back home.

Stomping through the door and into the house, before I could reach the stairs, I heard Mom crying in the living room. She quickly engulfed both of us into her arms and began to cry more intensively.

"She's gone! She died," Mom screamed accidentally; she wailed piercingly. Embraced in her quivering arms, I was numb. I wasn't sure how to feel. My eye moved spontaneously throughout the room. What I remembered most about this specific time was when I looked through the open window of the living room. I could see that the neighbors who heard Mom were beginning to come out. Though hearing such a scream, their faces said that they did not come out to comfort her, but instead, at 3pm, came out with looks yelling, "Shut that midnight cat up!"

Ms. Darlene had died peacefully in a habitual nap she always took about this time every day. I tried to avoid asking where we were going to live. It was the wrong time to wonder that as tears leapt from Mom's eyes and then Willie's, too. Again it was the generosity of Ms. Darlene that continued to shine even after her death. The shine she provided was necessary for the coming days that shortly followed.

6

THE TIME LEADING TO:

Mom had soon told us that Ms. Darlene left the house to us in her will.

"You are my family," Ms. Darlene would always personally confirm to me when I would sit down next to her in the living room during each of those separate late weekend nights. "You are my family," was always how she began the same conversation. Her memory had begun drastically fading over the years, but I didn't care nor did she care to show if she did. She had to have told me her story what seemed like millions of times, but because of her warmth, I never minded to hear it one more time.

"For years, the only understanding of family I had was the selective memories I have with my parents before I found myself on my own, and then with you all, Alex."

Every time she would tell this story, it was like watching your favorite movie or reading your favorite book for the 100th time. You knew how it would end, but there was still something about it that intrigued you. The first time she told me her story, I was nothing but maybe six years old. Since then, time after time again, she continuously told me the same story, but to me it wasn't the same story. The older I got and the more mature I became, the more I appreciated and admired the story that always followed her opening, "You are my family," statement.

After saying this, Ms. Darlene *always* paused. She would look towards the decorations on the ceiling while smiling at both nothing in particular but still everything. Every time, just before beginning her story, she would close her eyes and with finally opening her eyes, like one could not happen without the other, then also came *the* beautiful smile it seemed that only Ms. Darlene was capable of sharing. Several times I thought to myself that I could be 56 years old and still be as anxious as I always was to hear the same story I knew was soon to be told.

The period before her opening her eyes though seemed like hours. It was during this anxious waiting that I would notice everything that eventually became nothing to me, too. I noticed the things that I had long grown accustomed to being around to the point that it took effort to take particular notice of, but during those nights, with Willie upstairs passed out and mom usually on her way back from work, everything seemed new. As I waited, there was always that silence that reintroduced to me everything that at any other time I felt wasn't any longer worthy or significant enough for my attention.

Ms. Darlene was a fan of green tea at night. During the silence, her steaming green tea threw towards me what seemed like a perfume Mother Nature took pride in producing. The scent was so powerful that if I, too, with Ms. Darlene, closed my eyes, I would imagine being close to the top of a mountain, just before dawn. Every inhalation of her green tea would provide me with the comfort after a morning sky's seduction. Sometimes further defining the summer time as I waited for her to begin, I would then suddenly, out of nowhere, take notice of the pulsating humming of the unseen cicadas. I remember always listening and singing with them when I was younger, but as time progressed, I noticed the beauty of their sounds less and less until again, Ms. Darlene would have me sitting there waiting for her to begin her story.

More than anything else, one presence I loved to be reminded of during this brief pause of Ms. Darlene sitting with her eyes closed was noticing how wonderfully beautiful she was. The last time I sat waiting to hear her story, I confirmed she was beyond beautiful; she was gorgeous, near perfect. She was the embodiment of the wine neither Mom nor she knew I had sneaked and tried one night. Her brittling hair showed her scalp, the wrinkles under the sleeves of her shirt and pants seemed to be separate paths leading to the same great treasure—her heart. Though she lost all but 7 teeth, her smile was still excessively welcoming. A person could never help but to smile back towards her. The craziest thing about her smile, was that it never went away—even after her death.

"Momma was killed in a house fire when I was a young girl. As crazy as this world is today, there are more similarities than you'd imagine to the world of your elders and me, dear."

While this wasn't hard to accept, it was near impossible to fully grasp and comprehend. We've read, watched videos, and discussed the history of The United States in various classes. Mr. Hodge said something that always pertained to this. "You cannot judge what you have not experienced." Despite this, I strived every time Ms. Darlene spoke, forging if I had to, to have more empathy as she told her story.

She continued, "You'd imagine that my family would have more respect from others than we did. Momma was a nurse and Poppa was a soldier. It was complicated though. There were several times during dinner when Poppa would tell us that though he disliked the country he fought for, he felt he had no choice but to do so. Every time he mentioned the country, a certain pain and anger always crept into his body and showed itself to the world through the constant bouncing of his legs, the shriveling of his face, and the picking of the skins on the sides of his thumbs until they sometimes bled. Saying nothing though, Momma would simply place her hand onto his and all would cease; every ounce of negativity and what I felt was hate would *completely* drain itself out, Alex.

"Right then, at the least, he would exchange a smile with her. Kissing her either on the cheek or the forehead, he would then look over to me and say, 'It's for the betterment of you two, my queens, that I remain a soldier. Someone has to fight for a potentially brighter tomorrow for you two,' Poppa would always remind us."

She always repeated this before continuing on with the remainder of her story by further emphasizing, "Alex, Poppa *severely* disliked this country, dear. Every single time he would speak of it, the same newfound rage could be seen and felt. Sometimes it was so intense that it scared me senseless, but even if he spoke of the country and was mad and would remain so for several hours sometimes, after that brief interaction from Momma, almost instantly, 'the beast was soothed' as Granny always said to me about Momma and Poppa. Doing this was one of the ways Momma showed me the power us women have," Ms. Darlene would always say with the pride of a Silverback gorilla though she looked like a twig already snapped in two.

"Let me tell you, us women have a certain 'power' often and in-tentionally overlooked by this society."

One of the first times I heard her say this, I was confused, but still interested; I was intrigued while anxious to hear and see how I knew she would soon explain this.

"Don't get me wrong, Alex, I've never nor will I ever openly say women are more important, but they certainly are no less powerful than our male counterparts," she always said with a wink to me.

Key word, "openly."

"We *are* the holders of life, but too many don't understand this."

I always nodded in response only because I felt that was what she wanted me to do. I wanted to ask her to speak further on this, but I felt it was something that was common sense to her. I simply nodded to avoid embarrassment.

"This all being said, the family took a huge hit the day we lost her. I remember that evening. During this time, there were a number of casualties and conflicts in our community, but we, or at least I thought, were immune to it. Again, Poppa was a soldier willing to die for what others thought was for the nation, and Momma was known and respected as a nurse who helped both blacks and whites. She, Momma, unlike Poppa, comfortably helped—blacks and whites, men and women alike—simply because she knew it was the right thing to do. She refused to turn her head away from anyone. Momma was a hero, especially to me, but not everyone saw her as that."

After the many times Ms. Darlene told me this story, I could tell she still was vulnerable to the pain of this memory. Mostly, she would stop talking only to look me dead in the center of my eyes. The first time she got to this point of telling me of her past, deeply looking towards me, I quickly looked away. I wasn't sure why, but it was something about the look she gave me that asked me if I was ready. My looking away from her that first time gave Ms. Darlene the answer that I wasn't. After that, during the first time, she quickly changed the subject as if the past 30 minutes of her talking and me listening had never begun and we were back at the beginning of our entire interaction late in the night.

"Have I ever told you the first thing you said to me when I met you, Alex?" was the path and topic she chose to take instead of further speaking about what she had just avoided.

Almost every time after the first time she did this, the subject would never again change back to where she abruptly left it. I'm not sure what it was about me that changed after she had told me the same story a number of times, but randomly, at that same point of her speaking to me, when she stopped and I knew she was about to attempt to look me in the eyes, I remembered this and had already snatched my head away just as I had done those few times before. After doing so, thinking this time was no different from the others, I waited until she would change the subject as she always had.

I waited, but there remained a silence. I looked back towards her and saw that her eyes had not moved *at all*. Direct eye contact had been fully made and I couldn't find myself able to break from it. Her look stabbed me through to my spine. Stuck, I couldn't help but hear her body tell me that I needed to hear what happened after the point she had always decided to leave off from.

I'm not sure anything at all had changed within me. I think Ms. Darlene just felt that regardless of if I were ready or not, there were things she felt I needed to hear. Though this happened years ago, I still remember it like it was something just told. That night, choosing to go deeper, before the transition to explaining what had happened to her mother, Ms. Darlene looked back towards the ceiling, closing her eyes and for the first and only time, followed through with the remaining, untold portions of her life.

"That day, Poppa and I took a quick drive to the grocery store to get food for the big dinner we always had every Saturday—baked chicken, honey roasted rolls, okra—and also get the ingredients for a sweet potato pie that only Pops could make. Poppa told me that in a dream, even God asked him how he made it!"

Me and Ms. Darlene had to catch ourselves because we laughed so hard when she said this. Though Willie could sleep through a war even if it was just outside of our house, we wanted to be considerate. She laughed more at the statement than I did. Though genuine, I laughed partially because I was tired and I don't think it would've took much at all to make me laugh.

Finally breaking from laughs to chuckles, and from chuckles to again submitting to feelings felt with the memories I was soon to hear, she again continued, "Like many times before, we were at the grocery store down a few streets from our house—it was walking distance. We had been there so many times that once Dad called Mr. Bo, the owner of the store, and told him we were on the way and by the time we got there everything we needed was at the front counter already. Poppa was happy that this could be done, but only tried this one time. Poppa told me that he enjoyed walking the grocery store aisles with me because it gave him personal time with me, his 'Darly.'

"'Fur,' I thought I heard a man yell from outside the grocery store.

"Just before getting our last item, and before I knew what was happening, Poppa picked me up and we had already jolted out of the store. Over the trees, I could see a thickening black fog that turned into a swiftly widening cover.

"'Call the fire department,' Poppa mandated to a neighbor.

"Though hunched over his back, I noticed that Poppa didn't even look back towards the neighbor he yelled at. I reckon something told him he did not have to, and he was right. I saw that the neighbor beamed inside his house. I was still unsure of what all was going on until we got to our front lawn.

"It wasn't 'til later, after I grew a little, that I was able fully understand what it was that I saw when Poppa and I saw the blazes that was there loudly fuming before our eyes. Our house sat there, completely engulfed, Alex.

"I'll never forget the red truck sitting there just in front of our house. I remembered that as we approached, one of the five men I remembered seeing there in the back of the truck looked towards us and yelled towards the others, 'Here he comes!'

"The only thing that out-sounded the screeching of the tires' rubber as the truck roamed off was one of the other men in the car shouting to Poppa, 'Show us how you intend to save this life, *soldier!*'

"Poppa flinched as if he was ready to dive head-first into the house to save Momma, but deep down he knew it was already too late. The house already began to cave in on itself as the flames continued to flourish towards the sky. I guess he was able to accept that him running into the house was painfully senseless and would do nothing more than take two parents away from me in the same day.

"What accented the flames covering our house were the flames burning a small cross laid across the front of our lawn."

Briefly breaking from the story, "You want to know one of the craziest things about this day," Ms. Darlene then, out of nowhere, asked.

It was a rhetorical question, because I said nothing to answer her but she still leaned back into the chair and continued to speak.

"I sometimes have to forcefully put myself back at that point in my life. I think about that day all the time, but sometimes, sometimes when I think about it, there've been a few times I forged the scenery. Everything else would be exactly the same. Poppa and I would be there running away from the same grocery store and while running, he would yell towards the same frantic looking neighbor, and after reaching the house, we would see the same men speed off in that same 'ole rusted red truck throwing the same sentence towards Poppa. In the nightmares, I would even feel the same confusion wondering to myself *why is there a cross on fire* as we waited for a fire truck that never came. It was all the same, but sometimes, in the remembrances and nightmares alike, as that day would replay itself, the difference would be that all this was happening at nighttime. During those replays in my mind, I would feel a November chill."

When she told me all of this, I got confused almost immediately. How she described all of what she said was only how her dreams replayed. This was *exactly* how I imagined the scenery as she spoke.

For whatever reason, the only difference was that I imagined it to be raining.

"Contrary to the sometimes subconscious forging of that evening," Ms. Darlene continued, "it was the complete opposite. While all this was happening, Alex, it was a vibrant August evening. Not a single cloud on all sides of the horizon. The wind was gentle. Birds sang gracefully. The sun was more peachy-colored than it was yellow. While I still wouldn't recommend it, that evening, while taking everything in, I sat there on the grass and stared directly towards the remaining gleam of a sun soon to fully leave us.

"I lost my mom on such a beautiful day."

7

It was only this one time that she continued to tell me about her life after her mom was killed. Of the, say, twenty times she told me of her past, it was nineteen times that she left out this specific portion. She also left out the portion explaining her life after all of this. Out of all the late-night conversations between only us, those other nineteen times, I was not told of what I now know was *all* of the rest of her past. Again, including the first time and the several that followed, she always began telling about her past only to suddenly choose not to finish the story. I always took that as her questioning my level of maturity; what she may have felt was my ability to handle all of the rest that she had to tell me.

When she finally chose to reveal the rest, she repeated the phrase "I lost my mom on such a beautiful day," emphasizing different words as she would repeat them.

"I lost my mom on such a beautiful day."

"I lost *my* mom on such a beautiful day."

"On *such* a beautiful day, Alex"

Each time she said it, her voice grew softer to the point that I mistook it as a signal that sleep was practically knocking at the doors of her eyelids and that she was soon to pass out like I was close to doing, but refused to—just as long as she spoke.

Just as I finally began to allow myself to drift, she continued, "Nothing was ever the same after Momma was killed."

Her saying this out of nowhere scared me, yanked me out of the relaxation I was falling into. Ms. Darlene had weird humor. When my eyes shot open, before further continuing, she had a small smirk on her face. Part of what scared me was that just like before, each of the past times she told her story to me, once she reached the point of stating the death of her mother and the irony of the scene, *that* was where she always shifted topics. That night though, the night she decided to go farther, I was nothing more than a lost person in the center of a forest. I had no idea where she would stop. After scaring me, still battling the desire to sleep, I forced myself to look at Ms. Darlene with what had to mimic an owl's wide eyes. The look she returned directly told me she was far from falling into any form of slumber.

"It was never the same, but I made do with it. I had no choice. We had no choice. To this day I always look back to those years she was gone. I didn't realize then, but as I became a full woman, I was able to find a blessing in the passing of Momma. Those years were still rough, dear. Once I was able to comprehend the specifics of that day—those men leaving the burning cross in our lawn—sadness quickly became pure anger. It wasn't for long though but at one point I came to hating anyone even remotely resembling those men! I was scared to share it with Poppa though. I wasn't sure how he'd react to me saying this. He already disliked the same United States he fought for. I could only imagine. To me at least, it was *them*, the people claiming to have the most pride in the United States that took my Momma away.

"Nothing was ever done about it. Neither the fire department nor the local sheriffs came that night. When the sheriffs finally came the next morning, I could barely tell if they cared what had happened. They laughed and chuckled about something that Poppa and I were both sure had absolutely no relation to the tragedy that the burnt wood and dispersed ashes refused to let us forget. Alex, that day, I had never seen Poppa look so helpless."

Ms. Darlene continued. The room grew hotter. The heat I felt accented the hate Ms. Darlene had. It accented the helpless fury I knew her dad had to feel while the officers did everything but analyze the scene that contained the spread out ashes of Ms. Darlene's mom and the many years of memories. Without any rest in sight from speaking, I saw through sleepy eyes Ms. Darlene's hand raised in the air. It didn't register right away and it wasn't until I felt a sudden pound on my shoulder that the moment between us changed. It was no longer something desirable. The pound I felt travelling throughout my entire body brought something with it. I couldn't focus. Though it did absolutely nothing, I locked my eyes as if doing so would prevent tears from escaping. Cross-legged on the floor, my legs started to bounce as individual breaths became deeper. Still the room grew hotter. For just a moment, to see if she took any notice of what I was feeling, I watched Ms. Darlene's mouth continue to move, but I heard nothing. I couldn't hear, smell, or even taste the earthiness from the scent of Ms. Darlene's green tea like any of those times before. The warmth and joy of this moment completely vanished. Every bit of welcome I noticed those previous times with Ms. Darlene was replaced with the now rapid booms in my body.

This was one of the things that Mr. Hodge constantly told the class about. What Ms. Darlene was speaking about at that moment in her life was the dominant environment of the America she had no choice but to live in and endure. The same America Ms. Darlene's dad eventually died fighting for was the same America that freely snatched one of the most important people in her life away—without any repercussions.

"Alex, are you ok?" Ms. Darlene asked. I only read her lips hearing nothing.

"No" was what I wanted to say, but I said nothing.

"Alex," she said again.

The sight of Ms. Darlene began to look blurry. The room grew hotter. Breath intakes became shorter and sporadic. My pulse seemed to punch quicker and heavier.

Tears in a full stream, "Why," I finally mumbled. I said this after she laid her shaking hand on my arm—snapping my senses out of that state of inactivity. Her cold hands touching my arm brought with them floods of feelings.

What if Willie saw this? I thought.

I was supposed to be the strong one for him to look up to. I was supposed to be and remain the shoulder that *he* cried on. I tried to stop.

Failure.

Between the deep snorts from snot and racing tears, all I could manage to ask Ms. Darlene was, "Why?"

What blew me away though was what I briefly saw. I managed to wipe tears away before more succeeded in blurring my vision. At first, because of the interruption of tears, I knew I wasn't seeing things correctly, but wipe after wipe I accepted what was being shown to me. She was smiling.

Finally interrupting the smile she was wearing as I cried, "Because it had to be done, Alex."

What?

"Not necessarily that it had to be done, Alex, but from my Momma's death, I grew so much—Haha, almost as quickly as a weed in a garden, dear!"

I think you've officially lost it, ma'am.

As she continued to laugh, I shifted my body. I didn't want to hear anymore. I didn't want to hear this ever again. As I stood up on my knees, before being able to stand up, the laughing stopped. Her hand came back down. The bones of her fingers wrapped as far as they could around my arm, there was a grip that begged *stay a little longer, Alex. Please.*

Succumbing, sitting back on my heels, she continued in a murmur, "It was painful, Alex. That is one thing that I can never deny even if I wanted to. It still is, too. Shortly after Momma's death, as if nothing more could be done to further destroy the sanity I had left, Poppa, too, left completely from my life."

She stuck her chest out and made an effort to replicate a masculine deep voice. "'Darly, do you remember when I told you and Momma that it was your futures that inspired and gave me a reason to fight for this country of lunatics?'" Despite still contemplating how much longer I would stay and listen, Ms. Darlene almost made me chuckle when she tried to mimic his voice.

"By this time, I was about sixteen. We long left Mississippi and moved here to Knoxville. The only explanation I remember for why we moved here in particular, Poppa said, 'For people like us, anywhere is better than Mississippi.'

"'Darly, baby,' he said, 'there is war happening now and I have to go. I am leaving tomorrow.'

"Before I could say a thing back to him to combat his leaving, aggressively, only to show that nothing more was to be said, he demanded that I go upstairs to sleep. Lord, I cried something terrible that night, Alex.

"The scariest thing about that night is that I still remember having this gut feeling that coincided with the look that I could see Poppa giving me as I trudged up those steps right over there. I prayed hard that night. As strong of a man I knew Poppa was, the look he had when telling me this had sure fear behind it. I saw it and he knew I did. I kept asking God, begging that this fear seen within Poppa's stare would be nothing but a fear created from a possibility that would never be. That sometime soon, he would come back. To me.

"I couldn't fall asleep that night. I heard Poppa coming up the steps. Instead of going to the room on the opposite side of the hallway, the sound of his steps suggested that he was getting closer with each foot step. I wasn't sure what was left for him to tell me. Right now, Alex, you remind me of me. By this time, there was nothing left that I wanted to hear, but so much that I needed to still hear," Ms. Darlene softly said.

"There, blocking the light creeping under the crease of the door, I could tell that Poppa was right there. I was so focused and waited for him to walk in. I wasn't sure what I would say when that door finally opened. Nothing. Right before the door opened, I turned my body to face away towards the wall so that when he came in, I could at least play sleep. I'm still not sure why I did this, Alex, but I did. With eyes closed tight but ears opened wide, I could hear, feel Poppa standing there over me. For a while, the depth of the silence around us revealed that not a single move, barely a breath was taken between either of us.

"Poppa caved first. Goodness, did he begin such a cry. Alex, I had seen every emotion and feeling come from that man, but crying was never one of them until that night, that moment. It is sort of the same today, but especially back then, men had the roles of warriors, of soldiers, of providers, and all that mess. They were allowed to and sometimes encouraged to get angry to suggest that empty strength. Those that were considered 'weak' were barely, if at all considered men. Poppa, being a man, but also being a black man, always felt he had something to prove and thus strived even harder to prove his 'manliness.' Though the conversation never came up, I wanted to ask him if his desire to prove this was also a reason he decided to be a soldier. Aside from the betterment of Momma's and my future, did he further want to show America that he was just as capable as any other in being considered the social depiction of a 'man.'

"Over a decade of being raised by him, I saw just that. I never questioned if he loved me, but still the most affection I received from him was when he would call me his Darly. This all being said, there I was that night, eyes bolted, back towards Poppa, listening to—being that it was coming from him—an unfamiliar sound. Even if I wanted to, I found myself unable to move. All I could do was listen to the whimpers, until he began to speak.

"'Darly, I'm sorry. I've not been the same Poppa since we lost Momma. She was a significant part of me, of us.'"

Ms. Darlene suddenly stopped to check if I was still following. "Are you still ok, Alex? Have I told you too much?"

Captured all over again, "No ma'am."

Now smiling, "What he told me that night helped me become who I am today, dear.

"In between spurts of agony, he found himself able to continue, 'Many times I questioned if I could continue without her presence. Those nights without her sleeping next to me, those dinners without her prayers, but more than anything else, the power I failed to fully realize she had until she was no longer with us. I have been the soldier of the family, but she was the warrior. Several times she came home crying without you knowing, Darly. At separate single moments within separate single days, she endured what only a person as powerful as her could handle; from working the hospital, she would tell me of the births, deaths, and even the death threats she often witnessed—sometimes all in the same day! Several times I begged her to stop. I tried to convince her that if necessary I would pick up a second hustle to accommodate. Every single time, she told me that just as I had the responsibility of showing you the strength of a father, she had the responsibility to show you the strength of a mother, of a woman.

"'Damn did she do that well, Darly! Though she said she had the responsibility to show *you* the strength, I, too, was learning. Darly, *she*, not I, she was the warrior.'

"Then he told me something I had no idea about. Poppa continued, 'I reached the point when I wasn't sure if I could continue. I wanted to quit. I wanted to quit being a soldier and overall, life in general. It was one day recently that I was enraged just before dinner. I was scared I was going to take it out on you through words. I hadn't yet, but the breaking point was already stretching and slowly tearing. Just before I reached down and grabbed the first bit of food, you clinched my hand and began to pray. It wasn't Momma saying grace for us, but instead, it was you, Darly. It was you that calmed me just like she always did. Your touch was no different than your mother's soothing grasp. As you continued with the grace, I couldn't help open my eyes and when I did, I saw her. Not only did I see her, I *felt* your Momma, my love.

"'Darly, I am leaving tomorrow morning,' Poppa then said, still crying kind of like you just were, Alex," Ms. Darlene said with chuckle.

"'At first, I was petrified,' he explained to me. It was almost as if he forgot that I was supposed to be asleep, Alex. Still, he continued telling me, 'but when you grabbed my hand that night at dinner, I realized that in you is that same warrior spirit that your mom had. I've set up a few things for you, to help you after I leave.'

"Out of nowhere, just before I was able to finally find the strength to get up and hug Poppa that night, it all became nothing, again, when he told me, 'Darly, this house is yours.'

"When he said this, unable to prevent this, I took a deep inhale in response, but chose to still play as though I was asleep out of a pointless fear that became the worst regret I hold onto to at this very moment, Alex. I wondered if he noticed this?

"All he did though was finish with saying, 'I wish there was more, but I *know* you will be ok. I *know* that you will one day be seen and recognized as I do towards you and the same way I did towards Momma. Times have never been easy for us, and probably they never will be, but Darly, you are a warrior.'

"He was done after saying all this, Alex. He was done, but stayed in the room sitting at the foot of my twin bed. He was done, but still I played to be sleep. After he released all of those balled-up feelings, he was done crying. My heart started beating as he got up, hearing the bed screech and feeling the bed lift from where he sat. Poppa leaned down and kissed me on my forehead and headed out of the room.

"As the last words to ever be heard from him, before shutting the door, Poppa whispered, 'Darly, baby, I love you.' Ha! Cliché right?" Ms. Darlene laughingly yelled as she leaned closer towards me.

"Despite the prayers before and the prayers I would say long after he left that night, the last image I have of Poppa is that one of him still there at the table, one arm over the top while leaning against the chair. He was still looking down at the plate hosting food yet to be touched by him. His striped button-up shirt was untucked and crazy wrinkled at the bottom. His leg was folded on top of the other, but still under the table. It wasn't hot in the room, but sweat still glistened on his dark-chocolate face. His head slightly tilted down with eyes shut, but not tightly, these are the things I still remember seeing just before I reached the top of those steps. It was just under a year and four letters later that what Poppa had feared—that fear that could be felt when he came to my room—became a reality, Alex."

That night, she said nothing more. That night, she had already told me more than she ever had and ever would again. The few remaining times I would sit down next to her on those late weekend nights, I would listen as she'd begin to tell me of her younger days as though there was something new to tell—which there never was. The few things there were still to learn of her would briefly come with short conversations had between me and Mom. Despite the pain she endured year after year, it remains amazing to comprehend how it was possible for her to become *the* Ms. Darlene. The warrior I saw that night and still remember.

In the living room that night, I sat for over an hour after she stopped speaking. I was still taking in all that she told me. Several times I acknowledged how sleepy I was, but my unfulfilled anxiousness to hear more kept me awake. For what had to have been over an hour, neither of us were asleep, but still neither of us said anything within the passing time. I remember that for a quick second, fear outdid both my sleepiness and anxiousness. I noticed that Ms. Darlene had not moved a single inch. Whether or not she was breathing seemed to be nothing more than a gamble. While open, her eyes were locked; her eyes were stuck looking at the ceiling like they always would be just before she would continue on with telling more about her past.

"Ms. Darlene," I said in a whisper that made the silence of that night seem overpowering, unbreakable.

Though not immediately, her eyes finally blinked.

She is alive was a thought that brought alleviation,

"Yes, dear?"

Stuck. I hadn't thought that far ahead. Me calling her name was only done to make sure she was still alive. "Why did you take us in?" I didn't notice those words were coming out of my mouth. The question was spontaneous, almost reflexive. Up to that point of the night, it was a question I always wondered. *Why did she take us in?* The dumbest person in the world could still tell that there was very little that we were able to contribute or give back to her for the generosity she shared with us. I couldn't imagine what our life would've been like had she not taken us in. We had lived with Ms. Darlene for as long as I can remember.

Just after asking her that question I felt shameful. Fearing what I believed was the obvious answer, my head dropped with the thought that maybe the kids of the community were right. Maybe we were parasites towards Ms. Darlene.

"Goodnight, dear," Ms. Darlene smilingly said before closing her eyes to fall asleep.

After all that she told me, did she feel I couldn't handle the obvious answer? That was nowhere near the answer I both desired and feared, but felt I needed. "Because you all were broke bums," was not anywhere close to how she would've said what I wanted her to finally confirm to me.

If that was the answer, I knew without a question that even if that were true, that Ms. Darlene would never say such a thing though I did everything to emotionally and mentally prepare for the hearing of this—whether it came from Ms. Darlene herself or Mom. More than anything in the world, at that point, the answer to "Why did you take us in, Ms. Darlene" was nothing less than a natural wonder or treasure that I had been searching for years to find—though it was unknowingly at my front door.

Finally, the question was asked. There was no taking it back. All cards were laid out on the table and *that* was all that I would get in return as an answer that night. I didn't get mad or even that upset. To avoid any of that, I assured to myself that just like the many times before of her telling me of her past, maybe she felt that at this specific point in my life, I wasn't ready or mature enough to handle whatever the answer to my question was. As predicted, there came a few more times, personal and late nights being just me and her, there in the living room, me sitting next to her on the floor as she sat on her chair, me taking the time to notice all her unrivaled, angelic beauty, and lastly taking notice of near every single aspect of what always seemed like a new living room—especially that earthy green tea of hers, for some reason—just before she would begin to tell me, yet again of her past.

This one night of her going insanely deeper into the life she knew so well, for one time only, she broke the cyclical process that I came to remember. Though she didn't tell me that night, I thought to myself that just as the repetitive cycle was just broken and furthermore added to, this meant that maybe one day coming, at some point, she would again break it and go even deeper, and with going deeper she would also finally answer the question whose answer, like never before, I longed for.

"Goodnight, Ms. Darlene," I said though she had long ago passed out. She only told all of this one time. The remaining others were all the same. At the same point, she would begin to mumble fainting words until sleep would interrupt mid-sentence, mid-syllable of a word and she would sit, mouth wide open and begin a soft but still stone dry snore that sounded to be scratching the furthest top of her mouth. It didn't take long for me to accept that the whole process, the conversation, the telling me of her story, and her testimony became a cycle that would never again be broken. I grew to being able to predict things down to the pauses between phrases and words and the raw green tea, earthy scent of the living room. The repetition became sharply precise to the point where, if I had a better grasp of the passing of time, I'm sure I could softly snap my fingers in predicting when her open-mouthed snore would begin to faint and her smile, a smile that looked as if loaned by the sun itself, inched itself towards both sides of her cheek bones.

Ironically, as Ms. Darlene slept, she comfortably wore that same smile that couldn't help but tire-out and hurt my face the times I'd managed to maintain a smile like hers. For what seemed like hours into the night, even as she snored, she would wear the same smile— face wrinkles stretched to the point where her skin looked like nothing less than the same thin sketching paper Willie would use to recreate his favorite cartoon characters. Her face barely looked anything more than a professional paper-maché skeleton there patiently waiting to see another passing shooting star.

Unfortunately, I couldn't have been more wrong that night. She never personally told me the answer to my question. I never asked again, but still hoped that she would feel my yearning for the answer. The remaining times she told me of her past, she never again went deeper or even as deep as she did that night. Once or twice she added a portion to the story that she hadn't before mentioned.

"There was a boy named Elisha I met when I was about eighteen. Lord, he was something I thought God crafted Himself. He was such a hunk!" But it was nothing deeper than a random statement like this.

I enjoyed when she would add something to the story she had many times previously told me, so I always waited and wanted more. The portions of her life she would randomly add were only specks of a log compared to what I wished she would tell me. I almost wondered if she knew what she were doing. Mom always reminded me that Ms. Darlene's memory was fading. Despite this though, I witnessed on different occasions the reactive effects of her fading memory. When it came to her telling me of her past, over the years I often felt that deep down in this portion of her mind, she still had complete control. I felt that she remembered *exactly* what she had told me the last time and then the time before that and the many times before that. I felt that not only did she remember what she had told me before, but she already knew what she would tell me the next time, if and when that coming time came.

It was that feeling and questioning of whether or not the time finally came that the repetition embedded in our personal nights together would again be broken. Though I was ready to listen a million and two more times, I was most ready for when she would finally provide me with what I wanted most.

Though it never came, instead of losing interest, I always felt myself growing more interested and anxious every time she would start to speak—listening to every word twice as carefully as I had the time beforehand.

"Why, Ms. Darlene?"

It was a question I wastefully—though not regretfully—waited to be answered. She never told me.

I knew what she had told me then was not the whole story. Though I didn't know it then, it was the last time I would be able to hear Ms. Darlene tell me of her past. That last time she told me of her story was similar to many times prior to where she left out that huge portion of her life she had told me only one time. That night, there she sat with her head tilted back, already breaking the brief snoring phase that always came at the beginning of her sleep. The smile that was always etched on her face greeted me. With her stillness, she seemed nothing more than any other item in the room capable of being personified. Instead of waking her up, I simply turned off the light and laid beside her within the open space of her chair in an effort to reach the same peace that her smile suggested was reachable—reachable for even a person like me.

8

omorrow is the day, Alex

I kept reminding myself. It was a thought suffocating my mind. It was the only sentence that my mind decided to repeat excessively. It was almost like I was trapped within a gate in a dark room of my mind. Shadows of other thoughts could be seen pulling, grabbing, and beating against the gate wanting to get in and to me. I couldn't tell which desire was stronger, their desire to get to me, or my desire to leave out towards them. Within the silhouetted embodiments of the separate shadows, I could just barely see the thoughts of school, East Knoxville, Willie, Mom, myself, our future. At this point, good or bad, anything would have been better to think about, but still, *tomorrow is the day* was all that was allowed to be seen and heard fully. Trapped, this thought was the only thing on the same side of the gate as me.

"Have you ever been to one?" Willie whimpered. I could tell he was two quick breaths away from a full-fledged cry.

It was *she* that was often able to erase negative thoughts from a bad day by simply showing all of that nearly toothless smile. It was *she* that Mom continuously reminded me to thank because of the kindness and blessings she selflessly provided to the family. It was *she* that gave me the understanding that some of the strongest people in today's world may not have a single toned muscle. The few times I found myself doing so, it was Ms. Darlene I prayed for because I always knew she was doing the same for us. I had no understanding what life would be without her and yet tomorrow, that would be the beginning phase to this answer.

"No I haven't, Willie."

"I'm scared."

"Of what?"

It's times like this I always prepared for; it was times like this that had made me who I am. Because it was needed, I profoundly desired to be strong and stern for Willie. He could barely get a word out of his mouth without stuttering between words. That night before, we were there lying in my twin-sized bed, but finding a way to do so without much touching. I knew my little brother well. Because he almost always had that chipper, delighted essence and energy about him—even during what I considered the rough times of our past— those few times, like this, were when that energy about him became completely depleted of any and all positivity. I knew without question that he needed me.

He had no one else to rely on for comfort. Even after having moved in and time passed and we were an official family, though Ms. Darlene told mom multiple times not to worry about it, Mom still self-mandated that she had to get other jobs. I still think it was a pride thing. She would never openly say so, but I could tell Mom felt obligated to show to me and Willie the necessity of work ethic and grit in regards to providing for the family—even if it took away the ability to often spend time with us, her children. It was the price she was willing to pay if it meant for our betterment. As much as I wanted to sometimes, I wouldn't, *could not* fault her for her decision in doing so.

Regardless of her absence, Willie still needed the emotional support that we both quickly realized was not restricted to only being provided by a parent. I made a promise to myself that I would find a way to care for him like I often wished someone would, but didn't, for me. Ms. Darlene was able, but only to an extent. Even during those nights together and the many we shared as an entire family, my thoughts never failed to remind me that we weren't blood. "There's no getting around that," I sometimes had to verbally remind myself.

"I'm not sure," Willie mumbled, "but I'm scared, Alex."

I swear despite my vow to be there for him and support him, sometimes I wanted to yell at him; I, too, felt every bit of what he was feeling. Though I didn't, for a second I wanted to release every ounce of fear and anger balled up inside of me.

I'm scared too, Willie! I know why, though. Ms. Darlene is gone. She is why we aren't living on the side of some street or alley behind Jefferson Avenue. Mom said she left this house to us, but what more will the neighborhood feel and say about us now that Ms. Darlene is gone? I'm scared Willie! When mom is working at night, it will only be us two. In the morning, will I have to wake us up? Ms. Darlene did that, but what now?

The gate in that dark room in my mind finally crumbled. When it did, inescapable thoughts caught me in waves. They were so loud; I didn't notice when Willie began to cry, but still heard as he continued throughout the night. I tried to handpick a single thought and scream whatever thought to him, but I couldn't. *I* had to be "strong." *I* couldn't show Willie that I also wanted to cry alongside and with him, but *I* was the older sibling; because I was, *I* had to keep him together even if it meant allowing myself to fall to pieces. As close as I was to letting tears overthrow my face, I managed to continue constricting them.

"Don't worry, Willie, things are going to be ok."

It was yet another time I took a gamble. The only thing keeping it from being a lie was the unseen slight possibility that maybe, somehow, we would find a way to being ok.

Though I couldn't see in darkness, even though my eyes had adjusted to the tint of the room, I still knew that that was what Willie needed to hear. I could tell he began to smile. With this, his whimpers became more distant from one another until they completely ended. Before I knew it, Willie was sleep.

The good thing about his sleeping was how heavy that boy was able to sleep. If there was a bomb that went off no more than just down the hall from my bedroom, I'm sure it still wouldn't wake him up. Seriously. All that the bang from the bomb's blast would cause Willie to do is shift into another position.

Not even two minutes after I knew he was sleep, I embraced him as if he were Mom; I embraced him as if he were the strong one of the two of us.

"I'm petrified, Willie."

Fear-filled tears began to race. Lumps of snot were continuously wiped from my nose. The harder I tried to not let things release, the more pain-stricken I felt. The room felt like a furnace though I had goosebumps from head to toe. The harder I tried to withhold, the stronger the pressure to release all emotions grew, and the more confined in my arms Willie became. I gripped him as if, somehow, his peace would at some point notice, reach, and comfort me, too.

I envied Willie. Though he probably didn't know it, I always had. I was particularly envious of him that night. Aside from always wanting to wear and feel his smile, I desperately wanted the same comfort Willie fell asleep feeling.

There was one time that I slipped up and Willie saw me crying. Mom had received a call from the school that I was caught stealing a pair of headphones from the teacher's desk. Before I was able to explain that I was only reclaiming my headphones that someone found, she was already there at the school with the fierceness of a monster's worst fear. She burst through doors in such a way that I noticed the school's secretary and officer flinch right there with me.

"Get in the car!" was all she yelled before turning back towards the car making eye contact with no one.

I wasn't sure if I would be killed at home or there in the car. I knew that if I said anything, even if what I said was "Yes, ma'am," I'm sure that would've been the last words to be said by me.

"You just don't get it do you, Alex? I'm striving to provide for you and Willie. I'm trying- I'm doing more than all I can do to make sure you two do not one day end up where I currently am. The supposed 'real world' does not start after high school for a black person. It has long ago started for you. It has long since started, Alex, but you don't seem to realize that do you? What you are doing now is influencing the portion of your life that hasn't come yet. But you don't seem to care."

Before long, Willie was in the car with us. I looked at him briefly and though he wasn't looking back at me, but instead looking down towards his feet, I could tell he already knew he'd be stupid to say a single word.

"I pray that you are listening, Alex and you too Willie, there is going to come a time when neither I nor Ms. Darlene will be able to ensure that you won't do whatever again. When we are gone and you are doing the same things, then what? Whether you realize this or not, Alex, Willie is watching you."

Her saying this made my heart thump one hard time in response.

"I'll make sure that Willi—" I started.

Stupidly, I interrupted her. I did so in hopes to ensure to her that I'd make sure, somehow, that Willie wouldn't do the things I had been mistaken for doing. Again though, stupid. Before I could finish saying Willie's name, her hand swiped across my face with such a force, I felt the lingering sting long after I ran upstairs and slammed my door shut.

I sat there almost crying like some new born baby. There had been several times before that when I reached a level of anger at someone, for whatever reason, I would begin to cry; this wasn't one of those times. She wouldn't listen. Sitting there on my bed, already sniffling before finishing the previous one, rocking back and forth, I wasn't even half as angry as I was sad and lonely. Mom's words hit hard. I've long acknowledged how hard Mom worked, but the price of her having to do so also allowed me to acknowledge my selfishness.

"Are you okay, Alex? I brought you some tissues to wipe your nos-"

"The hell you are doing in here? Get out!" was all that I said, but what I felt was confusion. For the first time, Willie saw me crying. For too many times to count, I had seen him crying before then and almost every time he cried, I was there to comfort him—because I was older and because I felt obligated.

He is not supposed to be the one comforting—was he? Only I to him. Suck it up, Alex. Now.

Similar to the pride Mom had, pride alone was why I yelled at Willie. Willie had every amount of care necessary to provide to me the comfort, the shoulder I wanted so badly.

If he sees that you need him for comfort, will he then lose his desire to rely on you for the same comforting. Will Willie then see you as the weaker one of you two?

My thoughts were nothing more than insecurities I always lost battles to. One of the things I struggled most with all my life was finding my sense of purpose. Why was I here? Why was I born?

"Child, you barely a penny over ten years old," Ms. Darlene said once when I told her my fear of being purposeless. "Are you still alive?" she questioned with her eyes only halfway open.

"Yes, ma'am, but—"

"Then your purpose has not yet been fulfilled or completed. At least that is how I look at life, Alex," she continued. "As long as you are living, until that pulse we have ceases to provide yet another portion to this 'orchestra of life' as Momma always used to call it, then you are still providing an essential piece to the rhythm. As old and brittle as I am, I *am* still alive. You cannot avoid your purpose—what some would call your Destiny."

Though this conversation only happened once, her words were engrained into me as if it was a critical portion of our conversations during one of those nights. I almost thought she slapped me.

"You are still alive, Alex?"

"Yes, ma'am."

"That means you are *still* needed for something—something," she emphasized before quickly drifting into a nap that evening.

Ms. Darlene's words took immediate effect on my perception of life. Not even five minutes after she fully drifted away, contemplating every single word she had just told me, suddenly, it clicked. I told myself that *I knew* why I remained providing a portion to this rhythm called Life. It was caring for Willie—by all and any means. Whether, at that moment, it was forged out of my desire for an inner comfort or not, everything began making sense. I had already done so much for Willie. So why not consider that my role?

Your purpose is to be there, to influence, to raise Willie. That day, years ago, and for the ones to follow, up to this very moment, that thought was often heard as a reminder. That day became the confirmation I needed. It was both a blessing to realize, but also a painful curse—a steep price worth paying.

Because I wasn't an emotional person did not mean I wasn't vulnerable to the piercings of emotions. With an extremely busy mother unable to always be there, a wonderful but still old woman hardly able to stay awake for an entire two straight hours and a dead father, it was I, I was the one who fully accepted the responsibility to raise Willie as if I were a decade or two older than him.

Would a child rely on a parent if the parent relied on the child?

I had to remain strong. I always told myself I could show no weakness to him. The only time Willie could become stronger than me was when I died, and that still wouldn't be immediate! Discovering, deciding my purpose in life was that double-edged sword that felt to be going deeper every day that passed.

What happens when you have nothing left, Alex—when you have given all your strength and have nothing more to forge for Willie?

That thought was always a thought I wished I could escape. On the contrary, the more I tried to avoid it, the bigger, the louder, the more frequent and familiar the thought became to me until a point came when it would become all that I thought. But in actuality, it wasn't the thought alone that I tried to avoid, but instead, what the thought brought along with it.

You die when you have nothing left to contribute to life.

Eventually that night, my tight embrace faded. Willie continued to sleep as if I was nothing more than a pillow. Not a single inhale or exhale of his was interrupted. I still felt that I was far from following him into a deep sleep. I had no fear of being careful not to wake him because it was probably easier to make a pebble speak. Sporadically, I kept having to shift my body. At one point, for maybe five minutes, I turned away from him and tried to fall asleep. *Fail.* I lay on my back for a second and hugged the cold side of the pillow. *Fail.* At one point, still searching for some sense of comfort, my left leg, while still lying on my back, found its way onto the other side of Willie mounted on the wall. *Fail.* Finding a way to make it possible in that twin-sized bed, I had to have shifted my body a hundred times.

I wasn't sure what made it any different from the other position; I found comfort. Looking like a straight twig, I noticed myself laying on my stomach. I no longer felt a need to move. Eyes closed, I finally began to fade until I noticed a lighter tint of darkness coming through closed eyelids. Annoyed, but interested, I opened my eyes and saw that there was light seeping its way through the space between the floor and the door.

I was so close to finally falling asleep and yet the second my eyes shot open, it felt like they opened from nothing more than a blink at 4pm on a Saturday evening. The sleepiness I'd finally felt left in an instant. It was possible that it was Mom downstairs. I looked for my room's clock, but it was not where it always was. I rolled my eyes towards Willie's motionless body. He always found himself moving things in my room or even just completely taking them.

I closed my eyes again. I tried to fall back asleep though I was no longer sleepy. *Fail.* It was probably time for Mom to get home from work. I decided to get up and go see if she was ok. I didn't always do that. Sometimes when she got home from work, I was still awake. In bed, but awake. Several times I deliberately chose not to go downstairs—sometimes selfishly and other times selflessly; sometimes I simply didn't feel like getting up from bed when choosing not to go and other times I considered that she's tired and had a long day—maybe she wanted some time alone to relax before falling asleep.

This time, I chose to get up. When I opened the door, the brightness of the light in the hallway was painful. I had to stand still for a second to allow my eyes to adjust. Before walking down the steps, I noticed Mom's door was closed. Her door remained open until she got home and went to bed. Unlike Willie, I was an extremely light sleeper. Not only did I not hear the cracking from Mom creeping up the wood stairs, I also didn't hear her going back down the steps. I thought about it and I didn't even hear the front door shut when she came home.

Willie's sleeping strength must've rubbed off on me. That or his snoring in my ear muted everything else.

My mind was trained to listen for the sound of the front door shutting. I took it as a notice that Mom was finally and safely home from her final shift at work. Still, regardless of Willie being right there, not hearing any of this was rare. As I walked, I made sure to press down harder on steps to make the sound of the wooden creaks louder to let her know I was heading down. I did not want to scare or surprise her.

"Is that you, Alex?"

"Yes, ma'am. How was wor—"

I've never before felt such a way. A new branch of confusion, right then, was discovered. When I reached the end of the wall and turned to finally see Mom, not only did I see Mom, but sitting next to her was Ms. Darlene.

"Ms. Darlene!" I screamed without any restraints or care of waking "still-body" upstairs.

"Shush, Alex. Willie is sleeping!" Mom said irritably.

"I know, but Mom, Ms. Darlene? Ms. Darlene!"

I stared at Ms. Darlene so intensely that almost everything else faded. It was only the two of us, again, sitting in the living room like those many times before. A flush of that green tea scent swept over me. The giggling of rustling leaves outside began to calm me. The warmth of the room fully caressed me. I stared so narrowly at Ms. Darlene, I didn't even take notice of when Mom left the room. I stared. I waited, but nothing had yet been said.

"Responsibility," was all Ms. Darlene finally whispered as she remained there looking up towards the smoothness of the ceiling.

"What about it?" I responded already impatiently waiting for her to continue.

She said nothing more as I waited. I was still in confusion. It finally hit me, *Alex, this is a dream, dummy. Ms. Darlene—*

"Is dead," Ms. Darlene not only interrupted but finished as she began to slowly nod.

I became fully aware that I was in a dream which meant I could turn this into a lucid dream.

You have full control of the dream now Ale—

"No, you don't, Alex," Ms. Darlene again swiftly interrupted.

As she sat there, she wasn't frowning, but was far from smiling. The rocking back and forth she was doing when I first walked in the room was becoming more obvious. The glowing of her eyes was the look anyone would give just before they would begin crying.

"Alex!" I heard someone scream as if they were right there in my ear behind me. I swung my arms in response, in reflex to push away whoever might have been there, but when I turned there was no one.

"Alex!" screamed the same voice again behind me.

I turned back towards Ms. Darlene, but she was no longer sitting. She was there standing next to the chair and next to her, holding her hand was Willie. She stood there looking down towards Willie, but he was looking directly towards me—as if he was looking past me, through me.

"Responsibility, Alex," she again said.

"You're the strong one, Alex," Willie then said.

"Are you ready, Alex? They're coming."

"They're coming, Alex."

"No Alex, they are already here. They've been here."

"By all and any means right, Alex? Are you ready?"

"Alex!"

The last scream woke me. I felt the scream. It was like a punch to my ribcage. The sun in the sky told me it was about 9 o'clock. Soft gospel was playing downstairs. I smelled pancakes and sausage being cooked. Willie was already downstairs and singing along with the music playing. I lay stuck in thought before I was able to get up to join Mom and Willie.

Who is here?

"And mom says I'm a heavy and loud sleeper? Goodness," Willie said as I made my way down the stairs into the kitchen. "I would've thought *you* wet the bed if I didn't turn and see the sweat that was shining on your big head, Alex."

I didn't say anything back. I barely heard what he was saying. I was still taking in the nightmare; I wasn't yet sure that I wasn't just in another dream.

"Alex!" Mom shouted to get my attention. It was the exact same voice I heard screaming my name in the nightmare. I jumped from the chair and backed up against the wall.

"Alex, what's wrong? Are you okay?"

I heard everything, but couldn't speak.

"Mom lay her hand on my face, asking again, "Alex, are you okay, dear?"

The chill of her hand, brought me back and calmed me. The chill I felt had to be what Ms. Darlene said her dad felt from her hands. I was able to look into her eyes. I saw concern, but I also saw pain that told me it was finally the day. She was unaware of why I was acting the way I was. To her, as far as she was concerned, she must have thought that I was acting as I was because today was Ms. Darlene's funeral.

"Everything is going to be okay, dear. I am here for my babies," she explained while looking back and forth between us. Despite the sadness her eyes told me she was trying to hide, she forged a smile; it was so empty, but I'm not sure she knew I could tell.

In a sense, I wondered if I was wrong to—at that point—see myself as Willie and see her as me. In the same manner, I felt Mom was trying to provide the same shoulder—the shoulder she needed—to me as I always tried to do for Willie. At this moment, just as I could've provided for her, could and did Willie ever see through my desire to be strong though deep down, I was on the verge of a breakdown just as Mom was as she stood there still looking back and forth between us?

"I'm okay, Mom, but are you?" I was able to ask her.

Her eyes widened and she looked away. Before she was able to turn and walk away, I grabbed her shoulder and pulled her to me.

She started quivering. I still saw her as me; it was the closest I ever felt to me.

"I'm okay, dear. Thank you," she whispered in my ear as her shoulders jerked once against my chin.

The only difference between me and Mom was, I saw then, that she was stronger. Who knew how long she had been holding in emotions trying not to show to us, her children, what I called "weakness." I envied her. Right then, she cried the same cry that I wanted to do. Selfish. Never had she done this in front of us, but still, stubbornly, never did I even contemplate that would I ever— voluntarily—allow myself to do this in front of Willie.

She was Mom. She was "the foundation" of the family. She was the provider. She was also human. Just then I felt an uncertainty regarding if this "humanness" was something I was running away from when I proclaimed "my purpose" of life.

No matter what, be strong, Alex. The irony.

Eventually, Willie came over and joined our hug. Of course he, too, began to cry. Though I felt the warmth there resting between us, I couldn't cry. Like no time before, this was a time that I wouldn't have minded, but still, deep down, I was still too insecure.

Right then, I had every bit of evidence that showed me that my insecurities were nothing more than self-crafted fallacies and misconceptions. There was Mom, for what seemed like ten full minutes, crying her eyes out on my shoulder. Her cries fluctuated from soft murmurs to hard inhales. A few times, just as her embracing of me softened to the point where she almost let go and seemed to be completely alleviated, there came sudden firm tightenings that almost sucked the breath out of me. As this continued, I noticed that my feelings for her did not change even an ounce.

The only change of my understanding and perception of Mom was that at this moment, she inspired me. She became stronger. As the parent of the family, she finally showed us her vulnerable side.

Again, while doing this, nothing about her image became weaker. I questioned to myself why then did I still fear showing Willie the same vulnerability that I'm sure he knew was in me? This would've been the best time to do so. If my perception of Mom did not change as she remained on my shoulder, would the same be the case if Willie saw me cry right then as well?

Yes, I thought, but I thought it unconfidently. I remained there, the only one of the three of us, wanting to, but still unable to cry.

Her crying coming to a soft end, "Thank you, you two." This time when she smiled towards us, it wasn't a forgery.

"No problem, Momma," Willie said.

With a half-smile, I only nodded.

Her smile began to fade as she looked out the window and told both of us to go upstairs and get ready.

9

THE ARRIVAL:

"College Hille Seventh Day Adventist Church."

Despite our connection with one another before leaving the house, despite Mom releasing every owned stock of emotion, she still was not done.

"I love you Mom," Willie said for the millionth time. As much as he wanted to, he didn't know what else to say that could potentially lessen the burden of sadness we both saw that Mom was bearing there before us.

After the many times, Mom's responses eventually evolved from, "I love you, too, sweetie," to "thanks, dear," to just a smile, and finally to simply placing her hand onto his hands while still looking out the window of the car.

Again, this was the first funeral for me and Willie. Of course we had both heard of them, but finally we would be able to distinguish between hearing about them and experiencing one. The only thing immediately telling us what we would soon be experiencing was the gloom we were told to wear. From our heads to our toes, we were covered in black.

"At least you look nice, Alex," Willie complained to me just before leaving the house and hopping into the car.

It was funny. In such a short period of time, Willie not only grew taller, but gained weight. Though we always had some dress clothes that Ms. Darlene had long ago bought us, we rarely, practically never wore any of them. The last time we all dressed up, was for an academic celebration at my old, but Willie's present school.

"Perfect attendance *and* First Honors? Goodness Willie, you are currently a professional nerd," I said to him jokingly.

He didn't find it funny in the least bit. I couldn't have been more proud of him that day. When we dressed up that day, his clothes were getting tight back *then*. We still had the same clothes. He grew considerably since that day and now, he couldn't even get the button-down, satin-gleaming shirt's top button in.

"I look like a black and white checker board," Willie exclaimed.

As sad as the day was and would be, it gave me and Mom a brief but much needed laugh.

"Or maybe I look more like an off-brand penguin!" Willie continued, all but yelling as he started to wobble around in hopes to continue to providing positive thoughts.

"We have to go, Willie. Can he wear one of your collared-shirts, Alex?"

What if I said no? I thought, but of course respectfully said, "Yes ma'am." My shirt was too big for me and yet was still a little tight on him.

"I love you, Momma," Willie randomly thought was an appropriate time to remind her.

Since leaving the house, she no longer sniffled, but every so often tears could be seen escaping. She put on wide and tall, black glasses in the car, but she wasn't fooling anyone. The sun was high in the sky and we had a deeply-tinted car. Had she put the glasses on before getting into the car, maybe we would have been fooled, but that wasn't the case. When she put on the glasses, it was already too late.

Willie's first time saying "I love you, Momma," though genuine, was also responsive. The quietness in the car was beyond melancholic. There was a chill that the silence continuously threw at us despite the heat of that day as well as the heat confined in the car. The only thing interrupting the humming of the car was Willie. Several times had I seen Mom come home after her last shift at work, but never had she looked so…drained.

"Will she be okay?" Willie concernedly asked after closing the house door as we walked towards the car.

I wanted to tell him yes, but I did nothing but forge a half-smile, nod, and look back towards Mom who had already shut her car door before we shut the house door. As much as I wanted to say something comforting to her, I thought sometimes it is better to just allow a person to remain distant for a while. I wish I could've relayed that thought to Willie because when he first told Mom that he loved her, while she said it back with a smile, her eyes grew so red—somehow redder than they already were. It was then that she pulled her sunglasses from the top of her head, resting them on the top of her nose. It was nothing but a few seconds that me and Willie took notice of a tear following where one had already travelled.

I wanted to place my hand on her shoulder and confirm to Mom saying, "You ain't fooling anyone with those glasses." While her glasses covered her eyes and though the lenses came considerably far down on her cheeks, they couldn't hide a single one of them. Without a single sniffle or even the usual jerk from a brief and sudden inhalation, tears broke free as if they had long been deprived from sun exposure. They fell in two precise formations; her tears fell in single lines from both of her eyes. The look on Willie's face shouted to me that he wanted to do something, but had no idea what to do.

He wore a look of helplessness that without words screamed to me asking for advice. Too impatient to wait for an answer from me—not that I had had one to begin with—Willie's answer to what could be done was counterproductive.

"I love you, Momma."

During the short ride, that was all that was said in the car. The more Willie said this to Mom, the less responsive she became. I'm not sure if she noticed it or not, but the less responsive she became, the more emphasis and energy Willie placed on his "comforting" statement. Now no longer saying anything but responding with nothing more than a nod, tears still plummeted.

"I lov—" Willie began, but before he could finish, I tapped on his shoulder and I simply placed my finger over my mouth to ask him to say nothing more. Though confused, with a defiant look, he complied. His look of helplessness became more distinctly defined on his face. I could see, more than anything else, that all Willie wanted to do was to prevent Mom from further crying. I smiled to comfort him, but kept my finger over my mouth. The remainder of the ride remained silent, but the tears continued and would continue without any sign of end in sight.

"You two ready? Let's go."

I grabbed Willie's hand and we walked inside the church. We had only been in there a few times, but now, it seemed so small. The College Hille Church was actually fairly large, but once we walked into the sanctuary, there was a heat felt solely from the presence of so many people.

"Why are all these people here," Willie slightly tippy-toed to whisper in my ear.

"The same reason we are here." Irritated.

I was just as surprised as he was though. *We* were *the* direct family of Ms. Darlene. There were times when as we walked into the house after school, Ms. Darlene would be on the phone smiling as she talked—a friend or to friends. I always wondered who she was talking to.

"We are blessed to be with such a woman," Mom told me several times—especially placing emphasis on this that time I got in trouble at school. Mom told me a number of stories of when at some point in her life Ms. Darlene had helped someone out of complete generosity. There were so many stories to be told about Ms. Darlene that she only once mistakenly told the same story twice. I thought I comprehended just how much and how often Ms. Darlene influenced not just us, but the community, but I couldn't have been more wrong. What we saw as we entered the sanctuary was phenomenal! The church was packed to its fullest extent and still behind us was the line of those waiting for their opportunity to see, for what would be the last time, the face of an angel.

Not only were there so many people already present, but there were many types of people. At every angle of my vision was there a different demographic. To my right, I noticed some of the black families with kids that attended either or both our schools but lived outside of our block, within the "rougher" portion of the city. There were blacks, dark, brown, and light, whites, pale and tanned, and others from what seemed of every possible race. Still looking around, I also noticed a few elderly soldiers. In other places, I saw what looked like nurses and doctors just as old as the soldiers; I wondered if these people in particular had any connection with and were thus paying respects to Ms. Darlene out of the respect they had for her parents? There was no telling. I was surprised to even see Mr. Hodge. For a second, we made eye contact. I said nothing to him. He said nothing to me. With drooping eyes, all he did was nod in acknowledgement that he noticed me. I wondered what his connection was to Ms. Darlene. I was even surprised to see a few of our immediate neighbors present.

While we moved in a line, step by step, closer to Ms. Darlene, my eyes were still focused on seeing everyone that was present. At the worst possible time, I grew selfish towards the rest of those that we were sharing the sanctuary with. Never seeing half of the people *ever* in my life, an epiphany made me wonder if many of those I was noticing came from out of city and state. If that was possible, it might have also been possible that Ms. Darlene's image and influence was regional, national, or possibly international.

You all don't know her like I know her I caught myself thinking a number of times. Instead of stopping the thought, I allowed the thought to come ten and many more times. *What's her father's name?* I thought looking at one old, but burly man. *Herbert.* Looking around and then finding a woman that looked about the same age as Ms. Darlene, *What was her favorite candy when she was a kid? Gum or suckers? Neither! Ms. Darlene was not a big fan of candy at all!* Eyes came across a man that was in a turban and a pure white robe and allowed my thoughts to ask, *If you know Ms. Darlene, what is her favorite col- Green!* I didn't even allow the full questioning thought to finish before answering. *Not just green, but an earthy-green.'*

"That is one reason I like green tea, Alex," I remember Ms. Darlene telling me with that smile.

Question after question and answer after answer, I continued wondering if all the people I managed to ask knew any of the answers. As I continued, the more selfish I became, until I found myself asking the same thing Willie asked me before we entered the sanctuary.

Why are all of you here? You all don't know Ms. Darlene like I know her. It's impossible for you all to feel what I feel. Why are you here?

I allowed these thoughts to continue out of fear. These thoughts kept my mind occupied. The more I questioned people the less amount of time I had to think about the loss; the less time I had to consider that this was the last time that I would ever be with Ms. Darlene. While thus far, the thoughts had successfully occupied my mind and kept me from thinking of what I was fearing, it took only a second for me to realize that the effectiveness, the successful occupying of these thoughts, was only temporary.

Several questionings towards those in the crowd and several thoughts racing around my mind eventually and completely and abruptly stopped. I found myself directly in front of and looking down at Ms. Darlene's still body. Every single thought that was in my head must have found a hole somewhere and escaped and ran without any desire to look back. For what seemed like an eternity, I felt and thought absolutely nothing. Even after I tried, I remained in a state of null-ness.

"She looks so... so comfortable and pretty doesn't she, Alex," Willie whispered to me.

His question made me shiver from an uninvited impulse of fury. *Pretty? Is that all she looks to you?*

Standing there looking at Ms. Darlene, the fully-blown vibrantly colorful Zinnia flowers placed along borders of her frozen silver casket accented by golden parts, and the enlarged frame that within it had a collage of pictures of Ms. Darlene with each telling a different story from a different point of her life, I took "pretty" as an insult. Ms. Darlene was *gorgeous*.

Being pretty was relative to the individual and their judgement regarding whomever, whatever they were considering whether or not they had a simple pretty aspect to them; I always considered "prettiness" as something that everyone had the potential to be. "One man's trash is another man's treasure." I always saw prettiness as a solely physical trait. A person could see a girl and know nothing about her and still consider her "pretty." Ms. Darlene was not just another being. Being considered "gorgeous" is a trait that takes time to develop. Being gorgeous was not something that everyone was or could even become. It was a portion of character that after time would blossom. If Ms. Darlene was a homeless person that smelled like she took a bath in a tub of the foulest piss, because of who she was, she would *still* be what most aren't—gorgeous.

Though it was only for a second, I was lost in time looking at the pictures of Ms. Darlene. Most of them were of the pictures that Mom had provided from the house, but a few of them I had never seen. It was crazy that pictures accented Ms. Darlene's body far more effectively than what seemed like hundreds of flowers or the shining glow of her casket.

In one of the pictures, she was in her work attire. "I always wanted to be like Momma, Alex," I heard Ms. Darlene say in the back of my head as if she were right behind me. I heard her so clearly. It didn't scare me. I knew that what I was hearing was relative to what I was seeing and also relative to things I remembered her once saying to the family. In the picture, she was wearing her nurse uniform. For 37 years, she worked at the local hospital. I didn't think much of her being a nurse until she continuously told me how much hell her mom went through.

Why, I always wondered, *of all things, would you be a nurse? Your mom was one of the best ones, it seemed, and still, she was disrespected by so many?*

The only thing that kept me from asking, considering who Ms. Darlene was and knowing what her Mom also went through, was the fact that I could almost clearly hear that she would reply saying, "Alex, don't think for a second that those years I was a nurse weren't some of the hardest years of my life. Just like it was for Momma, especially when a number of the families of the patients I provided service to—even some of the ones I *saved*—still looked at me with disgust as if I were nothing more than a measly mouse or roach. Regardless, Alex, despite the numerous times I was looked at with hate and the fact that those times drastically outnumbered times when I would receive humbled signs of gratitude, whether with tears, smiles, or shameful nods from those that were expected and supposed to dislike me, it was those alone that provided me with strength. Ha! Whether appreciated or not, I had a gift and ability that could and did save lives! Who am I to be selfish?"

I heard her say all this and more though I looked at this one picture there on the far left side of her casket for nothing longer than a second. There was one picture that had a sepia tone to it that was of Ms. Darlene when she was maybe two or three years old. She had a type of frown that only toddlers were capable of providing. Holding onto an extremely torn baby-doll, Ms. Darlene was wearing a frown that could only make people seeing it want to swoop her up with no intentions of putting her down. *Gorgeous.* In another picture I had never before seen, Ms. Darlene was slightly older as if she were either five or six. This picture made my eyes widen as my head bounced back in awe. In the picture, there in black and white, Ms. Darlene was cuffed by her father's left arm to where she was able to kiss him on the cheek. On Mr. Herbert's right side, his arm was wrapped around Lucy, Ms. Darlene's mom as she was also leaning forward to kiss Mr. Herbert on his other cheek. Ms. Lucy's leg was propped up as though she were a model posing for a new brand of shoes soon to hit the shelves, while Ms. Darlene's face was like a little piglet. Mr. Herbert's body was looking nothing less than a solid black pillar, but his face was looking as lovingly vulnerable as some would say a proud father's should. It was a perfect picture.

Only half of a second had passed with me looking into this picture and still it felt as though I had been studying this picture for hours upon hours. It felt as though I was in two realities, two different realms of existence where while the timings of both were drastically different, they still perfectly coincided with one another. Between the brief scoping and analyzing of each picture, I acknowledged both the half of a second that may have passed in one dimension as well as the hours that definitely crept along the other. Regardless of the speed that each picture found its way to captivate me, and the sentences of the story that each carefully but still charismatically read to me, I left every picture thinking the same word—*gorgeous.*

When there were no more pictures to look at but one last one, I finally forced myself to see it. From the beginning, it was *the* picture of all the pictures that held within it the most power to me. It was *the* picture that caught me off guard and gripped my attention with the firmest clasp. I knew that once I looked at it, it would be like a commitment there was no escaping from. It was one of the first pictures I glanced at but was the only one I decided to avoid. My gut feeling to avoid it came from both the whole "save the best for last" concept, but also out of fear and lack of readiness. When finally catching realization that I was at Ms. Darlene's casket and taking notice of the features and decorations surrounding her resting body, though only out of my peripheral, I saw it and instantly felt life flow throughout my body. At that moment, there was a gasp that left me without breath.

Between the individual acknowledgements of each of the pictures, sporadically, I purposefully glanced at this avoided picture. The first time, *that's Ms. Darlene and a few others not too long ago.* After the second peep, *Three people.* The third glance, *Two women and a child.* With my heart beating faster and heavier, the fourth time, *No, Alex, two women and two children.* Finally, with no more pictures left to prevent me from confronting this last one, I started out looking just below it deciding that slowly, I would look at it from the bottom up. Though I had never seen it before, I knew all that it had to say to me.

"You are family," heard so vividly from Ms. Darlene. I heard this so thoroughly that while I was looking at this picture and could barely see Ms. Darlene in my peripheral, I wouldn't have been surprised if someone had whispered in my ear that, at this funeral, Ms. Darlene opened her eyes, sat up, and said this before falling gently back down into a comfortable position within her casket.

In this colorful picture was me, Ms. Darlene, Mom, and Willie. I don't even slightly remember taking this photo; it made sense though. In this particular picture, Mom, a little heavier, was just two levels and tightenings away from reaching a full bear-hug with her arms wrapped around Ms. Darlene. Mom was still looking at the photographer wearing a smile of about 57 teeth. While not showing as many teeth, Ms. Darlene, despite the stillness captured within the photo's second of time, showed a joy that matched the happiness of Mom. Bounded by a thin sheet to the back of Mom was baby Willie—asleep. No surprise there. This picture couldn't have been long after his birth. He looked so fragile lying there on Mom's back with his eyes closed as if they hadn't yet opened for the first time. There I was in the front of the picture. As Mom was grasping Ms. Darlene, my body was almost completely turned away from the photographer as I was hugging Mom's kneecaps. While my back was turned facing whoever the photographer was, looking extremely uncomfortable, my head was turned all the way around watching the photographer. I looked both terrified and curious. How tight I looked to be holding on to Mom showed how terrified I was of either who the photographer was or at whatever was behind the photographer. I could tell, with the angling of my tilted head, that I was also curious as to what it was that I felt on top of my little afro—Ms. Darlene's hand.

It wasn't just the presence of us four that caught my attention to the point that wouldn't let me turn my head away from the picture. I also took carful notice that there behind us, looking as welcoming as it always has, was the house we've always lived in.

"That was the day we moved in," Mom said in my ear. It was those seven words alone that snapped me out of my stare towards the picture. I wasn't sure which dimension of time the majority of my stare had become part of. I knew I had not been staring at this picture for the hours it seemed, but the impatient grunts and excessively loud exhales suggested that for however long I was there, it was time for me to move on and allow the many others behind us to have their last opportunity to capture who it was that was worthy of holding the term "gorgeous" as an inerasable characteristic.

Regardless of the time shrinking between the individual grunts and the growing groans behind us, looking back at Mom after she said this, though she wasn't looking at me, but towards the same picture, her eyes and smile asked in a firm sense to join her in ignoring those behind us. Though I had looked at every picture carefully, Mom took notice that I was looking intently at this picture in particular.

"She hadn't known us long at all, Alex," Mom began to whisper as she still remained standing stiffly there behind me looking at the picture. "She literally saved us. Had she or we not come that day, to this very church, I'm not sure where we would've gone."

I questioned to myself. For the first time in a long time, I felt that I was yet again so close to getting answers I waited for Ms. Darlene to tell me each of those nights—even if it was only one time that she finally let it out. Mom said nothing more of this as we stood there at the front looking down at Ms. Darlene.

I tried in every wordless way possible to suggest to Mom, even if it was right there at that moment, regardless if it would've taken five minutes or two hours, to tell me more about this day being shown in the picture as well as the time leading up to it. Still, nothing more was nor would ever be said.

"Let's have a seat," Mom said as she bent down in between me and Willie, hugging and then leading us to the front row of the church.

People stepped up and people passed. People moaned and others smiled. Soft music was playing, but it came from a CD. So many people had already come that I finally took notice that the CD only had one song and that one song was stuck on repeat. It seemed no matter how many times the song repeated, the line to see Ms. Darlene was still extended past the doors allowing people into the sanctuary. After we had taken our seats at the corner of our front row, it didn't seem like an hour had passed. The line slowly dwindled until there was no longer anyone left to get one last view of Ms. Darlene. In comparison to the abstract growing and lessening of cries from separate portions and individual people throughout the sanctuary, the song—that I couldn't remember the name of for my life right then—from the CD was a paddleless canoe floating slowly away over the horizon, but then finding its way, in a drift, back towards us.

"It's going to be okay," I emptily said to Willie. Mistake. After hearing this, and feeling my hand rubbing on his back in a slow circular sense, he snapped back up from his crunched over position and began crying like he got all that he was waiting for, but just as quickly as it was that he snapped up, I snatched my hand from him and twisted my shoulder away from him to the point where I successfully avoided seeing what I could hear was coming from his sobbing face. I had nothing left to offer him but empty and hopeless phrases of security. Yet again, it was ironic that I had done this. The same thing I took notice of Willie doing to and for Mom while we were on our way to the funeral was what I had just done. The same, while somewhat selfless, unavoidably ineffective and hopeless strives for comfort Willie offered to Mom, was what I found myself doing for him. If allowed, the reactions would have been drastically different than they were in the car.

I was selfish. Had I remained there, looking towards Willie as he shot up after hearing what I said and feeling the comfort I was forging with my hand on his back, I knew what would've have happened. All he would've needed was a fraction of a second of eye contact with me to let it all out. I didn't foresee him crying loudly while leaning on my shoulders, but the moans tip-toeing in and around the sanctuary would have then been a head tilting's length away from me. It wasn't *his* crying that made me snap away; it was what I knew would follow had I remained tilted towards Willie as he shot up.

Some supporter you are, Alex.

It's not that I did not know what I would've done—cry. What I didn't know the answer to was how hard I would've cried after beginning to do what I knew I would've done. Just as possible as it was that I could have begun crying right there alongside Willie, a deep furnace of emotions I felt had told me that I could've just as easily stood up screaming and bolting out of the sanctuary, out of the parking lot, running down the middle the streets looking like a three-dimensional shadow in the all black I was wearing. It was a gamble that I folded to out of the fear of what the next card only *could have possibly* been; so right there I sat and selfishly pulled and turned away from his lean. I imagined Willie sitting there looking for a comfort locked far away from a grimy hoarder. I felt the selfishness of this until, just as I had done, I felt the tiny hands of Willie rubbing on my back in the same manner that stressed without words "It's going to be okay, Alex."

Feeling his hand, there was another opportunity, another gamble. As the rubbing continued, breathing became deeper. If I turned back towards Willie, I was still unsure of what would happen after our eyes met. The chance still remained that there would be nothing but a much needed embrace between the two of us joined with minor moans, but I couldn't ignore that on the other side remained the chance that in a matter of seconds, all eyes would be on me until I was out of sight and down the street.

Take the gamble, I heard a voice say. Though I decided to comply with the thought, when I turned, it was too late.

Fail.

When I turned, my eyes met nothing but the back of his scruffy-haired head. My focus was on his, but then transitioned to where his focus, as well as everybody else's focus now narrowed in on. The pastor of the church followed by two men walked to the casket and started a prayer.

"Our Father. . ." the pastor began, but I heard nothing else. My heart imploded. I watched as the pastor placed his hands on the top of the other half of the casket that remained up still showing Ms. Darlene. What I was seeing forcibly but effortlessly numbed the remaining senses. I could see the intensity of the pastor as his mouth moved and juggled between words as trinkets of spit dived towards and around Ms. Darlene.

This is it.

The pastor and the two men stood there in front of Ms. Darlene. For some, they were blocking what would be the last seconds we had left of seeing her. Now building up a sweat from the continuation of his prayer, though his eyes were closed, both hands were extended out grasping the golden rail that was there above Ms. Darlene's breast. As the pastor clenched the railing of the casket, one arm from both of the two men there just behind the pastor reached out, at the same time, as if they were programmed to do such. Both of their outer arms were stretched out and waving—no longer in the same motion—towards the ceiling, as the hands of their inner arms crunched up the linen of the robe on both of the pastor's shoulders in the tight grasp that I almost flinched from as if I myself felt the clinch of their calloused palms. Still unable to hear anything the pastor was saying, I took notice that spit could no longer jump from his closed mouth. The energy he was recently giving off suddenly cold-turkeyed. Sitting on the front pew, stationed just slightly behind where each of the men were standing, each of their bodies reached a point of being motionless. Seconds later, their eyes opened, their heads lifted from Ms. Darlene and looked towards the enormous picture of Jesus that was there on the wall bordering the back of the pulpit, as if they were waiting for the picture to speak. Clenching the golden rail even tighter, the end was near.

For the little time that I knew remained, I stared and waited as if at any moment, as if just two eye twitters away, Ms. Darlene would reopen her eyes. I waited, hoping as if there was a slight chance to see if she would wake from her deep resting. I imagined it starting with several blinks. After enough blinks were taken for eyes to fully widen, she would then take a colossally deep breath in and let it release. She would then slightly shift her body weight to her left arm so that her right hand could grasp the casket allowing her to fully raise her upper body. I waited. For just a second, I thought it was possible that she, if anyone, could do it and after having done so, having gotten up she would look around, noticing the light brown pillars stacked along the walls of the church and the golden windows in between each of them. I waited as if at any moment just before that casket was closed, the entire church would see her getting up, and as she did there would be a loud gasp blasting throughout the congregation. Eyes would over-expand. Even more tears than before would fall, her name would be questioned, God would be both called and thanked, and finally, with *that smile,* she would approach me—directly to me. In her white clothing with its pink accents, I would then feel her sandy-freckled hand rub against my face like so many times done before. She would call my name, snapping me out of complete shock allowing me to once again and forever more look into those light brown eyes I thought I'd never see again. Without having to say a single word, we would all leave the church hand-in-hand. I waited, but only in vain.

Fail.

The casket closed and as it did, moans turned into gut-wrenches. *That* was the first time I fully comprehended that Ms. Darlene was dead. She was not and had not been as they gracefully suggested, "resting in peace," in front of us all in her casket. Ms. Darlene was dead. She was gone. Inexistent, and so was a piece of me.

"Ms. Darlene was not your everyday person," the pastor yelled as he headed back behind the podium. He began this with force. His words slashed through the sounds of every cry bashing between the walls of the church. "Right here, *is* an angel!"

"Yes she is!" yelled a lady in response to the pastor.

"Resting here—" the pastor paused while looking towards the metallic gleam of the casket in a confused gaze. The pastor looked as though he were caught in a trance. I could see his eyes jolting back and forth. Stuck in a pause after saying only those two words, the pastor looked as though he was still trying to comprehend, as though he came unprepared to speak. "Resting here is the perfect human, Ms. Darlene," he paused and begin to wipe just under his eyes. He was a pastor, he had done this many times before. He was renowned in Knoxville. Pastor was known for his social intelligence and ability to articulate even impromptu thoughts to audiences. Considering the streak of light beaming across his forehead, I sat there pondering whether or not pastor was still tired from the intense prayer said before closing Ms. Darlene's casket or if he, too, were of the many still groaning from the punches and grips of emotions making their presences known to all.

"Members of the community, of the church, and also you who may not be from this area, Ms. Darlene was a woman of unconditional love. If she only had seven dollars to her name, she was the type of person that looked for ways to give you her seven and *then* two more dollars."

"Yes!" was instantly and continuously shouted by many in response to the pastor saying this, but soon silence followed in anticipation of what it was that would be said next by the pastor as he stood there saying no more, still wiping his face with the sleeve of his right arm. He remained there looking to be searching for what to say next, searching for the right words that would add to the momentum feeding the power that all *felt* was necessary. For nothing more than a brief instant, I caught him looking towards Mom. At this point she took no notice of this.

Many knew of the generosity and the relationship between Ms. Darlene and us. As the pastor gave a short but still genuine look of sympathy towards Mom, she was in a frantic state thrusting back and forth mimicking the quick and excessive motion of a four year old having fun on a porch's rocking chair. Of the series of cries heard throughout the church, it was Mom's that was consistently the loudest; it was Mom's cry that was full beyond capacity with emotions. While I felt a number of hands grabbing my shoulders and noticing about the same number of hands holding onto Willie, Mom was completely engulfed by bodies, arms, and hands embracing near every square inch of her upper body.

"Ms. Darlene," the pastor began after noticing Mom and her cringing of pain, "gave to those who had nothing! Church members, when two people give the same ten dollars who loves you more?" the pastor asked rhetorically using an old-timed lesson, "The person who has 100 dollars or the person with only 10 dollars? For as long as I've known of her," he started now panting heavily between words while still wiping the moisture from his face, "*the* gorgeous Ms. Darlene gave, without question, not just some of the desired food on her plate, but *all* of the little she may have had at that moment!"

Moans no longer existed after the pastor said this. Outdoing the grand intensity present prior to starting the funeral, moans turned into screams that began and continued banging against eardrums. These came, Ms. Darlene would've suggested, from within—came from the soul, the spirit.

"Yes," I even caught myself whispering to myself as the pastor continued. After every statement regarding Ms. Darlene was finished, despite previous thoughts that the cries could not get any louder, they continued to find a way to reach a newfound intensity as they grew even louder than they were in response to the previous statement that caused them. No longer were people holding anything back. Every single person in the sanctuary received the same message that this was their opportunity to release *every* pain present in their individual existences, and that if they took this opportunity to release this pain, in its fullest, that they would no longer, ever, feel pain, collectively. There then came unanimous compliance.

Just as moans and sniffles had transformed into full-fledged cries and screams, the time for a further transformation had once again reached the audience. Captivated by the throbbing agony over the loss of the precious loved one that now and would forever more lay within a casket, people started to roar. It was numbing. I wasn't crying, but my eyelids were starting to flutter and my vison was becoming a moistened sense of a blur. My mouth opened to also roar along with the already roaring Mom, Willie, and the rest of the congregation, but nothing came. It was not because I was withholding anything. The pain I felt was so intense, it felt like my body couldn't release it without exploding right there in front of everybody. The presence of my roar was felt just under my throat trying to squeeze its way out. I couldn't breathe. Releasing this pain was no easier than, as Ms. Darlene once said while reading from her personal Bible, "Fitting a camel through the eye of a pin-needle."

For just a brief moment, the roar of many bashing through the congregation, now also including the pastor, was interrupted by the ringing of a phone. It wasn't that the ringing was loud, but more so that it was completely unexpected and shocking. But it only interrupted the congregation as if, at the same time, people took a deep breath of inhalation; the roaring continued. The roaring continued for two more seconds until again, another buzz happened.

Alex!

Breaking the rocking I didn't realize I was doing and then reopening my eyes, I looked up already showing an innocent face striving to portray that the buzz heard did not come from me. I searched looking for whoever it was that yelled my name. After again being interrupted, the roaring ceased, but slowly began to again gain momentum in hopes of reaching the level of intensity that it once reached. Unfamiliar with what would be said or done even if I found whoever accused me, I continued to search for whoever it was that mistakenly called me out.

Alex! I heard again, but this time it threw me into a deeper feeling of numbness as my eyes widened. I immediately remembered that specific voice I had now heard twice. It was the voice of Ms. Darlene.

Responsibility, Alex!

The transition happened so swiftly. Not only did it seem like we were no longer at Ms. Darlene's funeral, the sudden swoon that struck each of us in the congregation, at the same time, made it seem like the funeral as a whole, the loss, the pain, the thundering roars were nothing more than being caught in a fear found while daydreaming in the passenger seat of a car. Once snapped out of that daydream, the grips the fear had fainted into the past and into the back of memory. Right then, I was there back in reality.

Though still in the sanctuary, though still sitting in front of a closed casket that within it held a jewel that would baffle even the wisest alchemist, though still in the pulpit was the pastor dripping with sweat from providing his most intimately profound service in a church, and though to my side and the rest of my surrounding were Willie and Mom, and the rest of those whose faces now had dried trails of tears and others with hands still faintly risen towards the ceilings, we were no longer at the funeral.

A series of phone buzzing and ringing began. Many were lucky that no one called, because as the majority of phones buzzed rapidly, a number of others gave off a siren-like notice which signified that the owner of that phone had forgotten to silence it. In a matter of seconds, the buzzing and siren-ing of phones grew from three phones to six phones, to twenty phones, to sixty-five, one-hundred and sixty-three, and continued until even the pastor, too, with a look of interest, submitted to the curiosity of finding out what was so important that every phone was notified.

I could see confusion. Shock was scrunching every one of the individual faces as cellphones began endlessly buzzing simultaneously. Aside from the basses and melodies still barely able to be heard from the CD still playing through the speakers, the phones were collectively interrupting the silence responsible for suffocating the congregation. Breaking away from the eye contacts of confusion shared by many, everyone soon complied. Just as soon as they complied and brought out their phones, the beginning of it all just as quickly made its presence known.

I remember hearing a similar sound while in Mr. Hodge's classroom once. The pulsing-buzz of his phone interrupted him in the middle of one of his predictable rants. His phone became its own siren until he finally took hold of it. Mr. Hodge taking notice of his phone said enough; it took a lot to break his always intense focus while speaking to our class. For example, there was a time he had not noticed to the principal walking in. There was another time Mr. Hodge didn't even see the city mayor walk in while visiting individual classes at the school. Though he had not said to the class anything that could get him in any trouble, the shock that struck his eyes after finishing his rant and finally noticing the mayor revealed to us all that to him, it was as if she had walked through a wall or appeared out of the thinnest of any air known to man.

The time he took out his phone, he finally looked up to inform us, "Class, a young girl has recently been abducted and is being searched for."

Remembering this, while there in the congregation, thinking as people began reaching for their cellphones, I wondered, *Who has been abducted now? What if the president was killed for the fifth time in human history? Don't county systems sometimes do random testing on phones to ensure to the owners, as well as themselves, that the notice system is still in effect and will immediately notify them if and when anything happens? If I am not mistaken, sometimes—*

"Get to your homes! Now," Screamed the pastor with such an intensity. Just then, he alone seemed to be able to mimic the rattle effect from the previous roaring that had taken the entire congregation ample amounts of time to reach.

Within the College Hille Church, Hell broke loose. For the first and only time in my life, I reached this… mental empowerment. I was in a state where after I hopped to my feet, as a reflex shared with the majority of the rest of the congregation, I was able to see and take notice of *everything* around me. I was able to do this without even slightly tilting my head or twitching my eyes. I found myself in a state of mind that, with the collaborative screaming felt, caused my ears to twiddle from every individual wave of sound that reached me. I heard the frantic words of fear from those already out of the doors of the sanctuary and already at the doors of their cars. Stuck there staring directly at the casket and its stillness, but somehow taking in everything around me, I still saw the tumbling of people bum-rushing any and everybody that stood between them and the exit doors.

"Did the call say how many there were?" I managed to hear a random voice hysterically question somewhere in the mass of raging people.

"Do we have time to pick up your mother, Evelyn?" I heard a soft voice scream.

Off in a corner, I saw Mr. Hodge. I wouldn't have been surprised if I saw him become one of the bulls marching through the doors, but in the midst of the chaos, I looked next to him and saw that he was there, bent over embracing a crying girl. He was looking back and forth as if there were some hope of being able to take the slightest notice, pinpointing any one person that seemed to be looking for their lost daughter.

Rows behind us was an old black lady still sitting. Though there was a thin drape attached to her black hat that curtained over her face, I could still see her lips quivering as she spoke in tongues. Her eyes were fully rolled back and she, close to the stiffness of rigor mortis, bounced on and off the back of the pew.

This is last America!

"We're not gonna make it!"

"Alex!"

"Know that I love you, dear!"

"Honey, please tell me… the gun… still in the car?"

"Alex!"

"Is *that* them!"

I could hear and see all, yet took little notice of when exactly I had been yanked off my feet and into a drag. With Willie over her shoulder and her other arm pulling me as if I were a pillar Sampson was chained to, we, too, were of the ones now in a rampage to the doors. Loads of people were crunched over or fully laid out in the aisles of the church as if they long ago reached that final point of living. Though quickly moving towards the exit, off of gut reaction, I focused in to where I remember seeing Mr. Hodge and the little girl. At that point, with what seemed to be the dancehall of demons prancing all around, I wasn't sure if *not* seeing them was a good or bad thing.

Just before reaching the exit, being able to take one last notice of what it was that we came for, the funeral, in only a matter of seconds, everything had changed. The intimately-yellowed windows were broken; some with minimal holes at some corner of the window's frame, while others looked as if full bodies had plunged at and straight through them—a possibility. Some of the darkened pews, in a few of the rows, were either pushed against or fully leaning onto the row behind them. Scrunched-up bodies were now mounds of unconscious bodies. Rugs were flipped over, cushions were torn, and every essence of love for and or remorse for and towards Ms.

Darlene was far absent. Cutting the corner of the sanctuary's door, the last thing I took notice of before losing sight of all that remained in the sanctuary was, though still closed shut, the casket of Ms. Darlene that had been kicked over onto the ground at the quick beginning of this rampage.

Outside was no better than what was inside the church. In reality, starting after the first buzz, which was the first interruption of the funeral, no more than three minutes had passed before we were swept up and dragged out by Mom. Three minutes was all it took to transform one of the most respected and renowned sanctuaries of Knoxville into what looked like a building that was part of an area belonging to the heart of a decade-deserted ghetto. What was seen outside was what remained from the first quick sweeping touchdown of destruction. Fumes of gas tainted the air I inhaled. Cars were totaled and left behind in the middle of streets that further prevented the passing of any cars wanting to go certain ways. Looting from neighboring local stores had already made its presence overtly known. In no more than three minutes, sirens of every emergency vehicle could be both seen rushing down blocks in every direction and could be further heard, in abundance, miles away. Small and separate waves of families were running hand in hand; some into homes across the street and others running until they would never again be seen. Three separate times I heard gunshots sprint down the streets until transforming into nothing more than echoes.

Why?

"People don't care until something is at their front door knocking," I remembered Mr. Hodge saying.

In the backseat, I was just there. Willie, mouth trembling and eyes closed so tight his eyebrows looked as if they were one in the same as his cheeks, was curled up and jittering as if he were naked and outside and trapped in a 27 degree night with furious winds. There in the back seat, Willie was a victim of sudden shell shock. Better yet, Willie reminded me of the elderly woman I saw before exiting the sanctuary that was left speaking in tongues. I didn't waste my time wondering ways to comfort Willie. How could I? I couldn't help myself. From a sudden turn Mom must've had to do, I rolled from the backseat onto the floor of the car. It wasn't just that I chose not to get up from the seat, I couldn't. I didn't want to see anymore. If I were able to, I would have left the reality that was happening on the other sides of the windows.

Closing my eyes, I tried to incarcerate myself into any deep thought that would allow me to escape. I tried to focus on pleasure, pain, fear, and any other specific feeling or thought that would grant me a ticket for the quickest trip away from all that was happening. It seemed that every time I made the simplest of any progress of drifting away into the utopia that was somewhere deep in my mind, it was sporadically interrupted by me hitting my head on the door as a result of Mom having to make an abrupt turn.

"My God. My God. My God," was all that Mom kept whispering between her gasps for air.

Regardless of being in a position where I was uncomfortably on the back of my left shoulder facing both the top of and front of the car, I refused to get up and see all that she was seeing. I couldn't see the front of Mom's face, but the constant and sudden shifts of her head and the mountainous goosebumps glowing from the sweat on her said to me all that I needed to be told. She was scared. That was a weird thing to acknowledge coming from Mom. She never feared. Especially because of her commitment to Christianity, though sometimes she worried, sometimes she got anxious, and while other times she was concerned, "God has it all under control," was always all that she needed to repeat to herself. That was all she needed to tell herself to avoid the feeling of fear. In the car though, fear fully consumed her. Fear seemed to have done away with every other possible thought and emotion. For only a second, acknowledging the fear I knew she was feeling was strong enough to captivate and focus my mind and take me away from all that was happening, but a suddenly rigid swerve to the left threw me hard into the door—this time sending an agonizing pain sprinting up and down my neck. Hearing an ambulance's siren quickly approach and zoom by yanked me back into what I came to terms with as the unfortunate reality I had found myself trapped in indefinitely.

Despite this all, for a just a second, I was able to see a certain something. Even while considering the many conversations had and the several times she found a way to make an event of her life relative to my life, it was during all of this time in particular that I had never felt closer to Ms. Darlene. It was the weirdest irony. I was unable to say anything and was barely able to move while taking in all that was happening. I was caught in a trance that bound me to searching for a treasure box that within it had *the* answer pertaining to every question I had. It made no sense. It was taking in the irony that finally allowed me to completely escape into a realm of deep thought. It was after that last tire-screeching turn, the passing of the siren, and the involuntarily seeing outside of the window that allowed my escape to begin.

During all of this, there was still not a single cloud in the sky unless from something that was on fire. The sky looked like a palette that warm colors had been thrown onto it in a particular way and order that made the point of distinguishing the deep yellow, full orange, faithful red, and every possible tint of the intimate colors almost impossible. In a sense, the colors were nearly indistinguishable from one another. Amongst the other natural beauties that contradicted all that was happening, it was the sun that blew my mind away.

Is this what you saw Ms. Darlene, I thought and waited for an answer—still stubbornly refusing to accept that she was dead.

I thought of the conversation we had, when she told what everything looked like when she saw the housing burning under the evening sky. I took notice that the sun was providing a shine that was so welcoming. The sun remained there, vibrantly, despite all that was happening to those around me, whether they noticed it or not; regardless of whether they were feeling the sun's 85 degree embrace or not, the evening alone was beautiful.

I see now what you saw then, Ms. Darlene. Regardless, still the sun smiles.

10

I woke up hollowed. After a twitch, my eyes shot open and I immediately began listening for any trace of what I last remembered. All I could do was listen because though my eyes had adjusted, night's darkness still engulfed me. Before thinking to inch my head to either side, I closed my eyes to focus strictly on what could be heard.

Before my eyes were able to fully close, the last things I remembered seeing came bashing against me in bright and precisely defined flashes. I instantly remembered College Hille Church, the pastor's sweat, the roaring of magnified cries, trampled-over bodies looking like lawn and street trash recently abandoned. Just as easily as these recent thoughts continued to rush into sight, they also left, leaving room for yet another and many more to still follow. Laying there motionless, eyes still closed, I remembered Mr. Hodge and the kid…the old lady stuck on the pew swaying. I remembered being unable to move. There in the darkness with eyes closed and stuck in a motionless manner, the only difference in being compared to being motionless at the funeral was that at the funeral, I was involuntarily motionless—I was in every sense stuck. Having yet decided to move, randomly, I had the epiphany that it was a soulful instrumental of "Amazing Grace" that was being played time after time softly before the service started and even more softly after it began.

Now almost fully captivated by the memories, my eyes now refused to open; my mind had mandated the necessity of remembering all that was there before passing out. As if I were at the funeral all over again, though right there, now able to comprehend being on a floor of a near pitch black room, I again felt the seven different hands on my back belonging to five people praying passionately while Willie clutched on to my elbow in complete confusion. I remembered hearing a gun shot, the heat and the grime from the humidity, the flocks of black birds singing as they danced above, the sun, the gorgeous golden sun beaming a vibrant intimacy uninterrupted by clouds unable to be seen anywhere above the horizon. I remembered Ms. Darlene.

It was then that my eyes opened. They didn't shoot open or anything, but just sort of solemnly lifted up. I figured that if there was anything significant happening outside I would've instantly taken notice, but that claim and thought, too, turned into nothing but a desire. Out of nowhere, I took notice of Willie's snore. The sound of it was like one of those days where Mr. Hodge was ranting. As he started and continued, usually I would begin daydreaming about something. Even as I noticed myself daydreaming as Mr. Hodge spoke, his bickering couldn't be heard as anything more than a humming portion of neglected white noise. As loud as Willie's snoring was when I noticed it, I thought it was impossible for that growling to start completely out of nowhere. I figured Willie had always been snoring, but it was just that the grips of the memories were just stronger.

I was back. I sat up crossing my legs. Eyes had adjusted to the darkness a little better. Willie continued to snore like some kind of bear in Gatlinburg. I looked closely to see if there was anything in particular to notice about Willie and started to crawl silently over to him. The cover he had was barely being used. Willie was just there on the floor lying on a soft pillow. He still had on most of the clothes from the funeral; aside from him lying there shirtless, he still had on the pants, the socks, and one of his shoes. As I was there bending over and studying his face, I hoped to see maybe the last thing he felt before dosing off.

A number of times in the past, after falling asleep crying, though I hated to know he had been crying, I always thought that streaks of dried tears on his face made him look like a clown that stopped preparing for a show. Looking for the streaks of dried tears that I knew would be incomparable to any I had ever seen on his face before, as I got closer, at this point almost straining my eyes, I noticed that not only had Willie not been recently crying, but as he lay their snoring like some kind of exhausted gremlin, he had a slight smirk on his face.

Seeing this slightly helped me. I sat back down from crawling and took notice of where we were. Still hearing nothing outside, barely even birds or the ruffling of leaves, I noticed we were definitely at the house and upstairs in Mom's room. As easy as it was to overlook Willie's obvious snore, it may have been just as easy to do the same regarding Mom, and just as quickly as I thought that, I became as still as I was when I first woke up. Feeling that my sense of hearing could provide to me what I wanted even more quickly than getting up and looking over, immediately I noticed that I heard absolutely no snoring. I soothed my random feeling of nervousness after noticing this, but then it hit me. First, considering that hearing anything at all, aside from the growling happening an arm's length away, was nothing but a waste of time—impossible, and second, it was stupid to listen for Mom's snoring to begin with. Ms. Darlene always said that Mom worked so hard that she didn't ever have the energy to even snore—which I accepted because she truly rarely snored or at least, if she did, she snored at a volume that could barely be heard.

While Mom wasn't a snorer, she didn't always sleep in stillness. Taking this into consideration, also questioning myself as to why I didn't just get up and go over, starting completely over, this time I listened and held my breath in an effort to prevent even the slightest sounds that could interrupt my hearing of Mom's movements in the bed. Even the softest movements on top of her silk-shining sheets would be considered bangs in this particular silence. I was listening with such focus. Instead of my eardrums, it was the banging of my heart's thumping rhythm that came without any care regarding whether or not I was ready. I heard nothing. Finally grasping what common sense told me I should've done to begin with, instead of contemplating what else I could listen for, I sprung almost completely off my butt onto the side of the bed only to see that Mom was nowhere in the room.

Is she dead? Did they kill her? Who are they to begin with?

These were both the first and the worst thoughts I could've possibly heard my mind whispering. These did nothing but push me into a further state of worry than I remembered passing out in. My palms began sweating. My left eye thumped twice. Though in the same cold room I remembered waking up into, I felt confined within the heat of twelve quilts. I took a step from the bed and noticed three things. The first was the usual creak that came from stepping on certain parts of the wooden floor of the house. The second thing I took notice of was Willie's reaction to the sound of the creak. It seemed to have disturbed him. After having heard it, his snore was discontinued, his smile was swiped away and abruptly replaced by a mug and then a frown that scrunched his face up. That expression lasted only a full second before the smirk came back and remained there as if ingrained. The third thing I took notice of was a slight change in the white noise I was already familiar with. Nothing was added to it when I focused in on my surroundings yet again. Instead, it seemed as though something was taken away. Something was taken away from the white noise heard in the back of my mind and just as quickly as I questioned myself *did it come from downstairs?* I had already bolted out of the room and was halfway down the steps.

Is she dead? Was the only thought I heard as it was played at least a thousand times within the two seconds it took me to get to the bottom of the steps. There at the bottom, I stood listening and looking for the slightest clue that would allow me to confirm that Mom was still alive. At the bottom of the steps, nothing. *Creak.* Similar to the one I had just made, I ran towards the sound to greet Mom even if, for whatever perceivable reason, it was for one last moment, for one last time.

Leaving from the steps and sprinting down the short hall, just as my right foot breached over the corner of the living room, before my eyes could focus on anything on the other side of the room, I was tackled. Between what seemed to be two neighboring milliseconds, I found myself on the ground, mouth covered, unable to see what or who it was that held me in an immovable embrace. I wished it was a dream like the one I had before the funeral, but the firmness of the hold told me it wasn't anything close to a dream.

"Say nothing," whispered the voice in such a grunt that nothing regarding who the voice came from could seem accurately imagined.

It's them, I heard my mind frantically alarmed. My heart began to beat as if the few remaining bits of life were being counted down. I could feel that my eyes became the size of two golf balls. Arms and legs were thrown around in hopes that something would've helped me get free. If this was how I would die, right there in my home, I wanted to at the least see who it was that was responsible.

"Stop moving, now," the voice whispered but also commanded.

In less than 24 hours, not only did unforeseen events strike our city, but right here, in my house, the same unforeseen was present. I imagined right before my eyes a clock ticking down regarding how much life I had left. Mom was somewhere gone. I was soon to follow her, and upstairs was Willie. *Would the same happen to Willie?* I started thrusting back and forth with all of the little remaining hope of escaping. The grip over my mouth, and the hug coming from behind clutching over my stomach only grew even firmer.

Why am I not gone yet? I finally thought and with this thought, all resistance left completely from every bit of skin covering my body. I was ready. *I could soon see Ms. Darlene* was something I began to accept right then and there.

This is it. I love you, Willie. I'll see you soon, Mom and Ms. Darlene.

"You can't be making all that noise when you come down the steps," the voice whispered.

I felt the grips loosen up in a sense that suggested that I turn around. There she was. Mom. Seeing her was the reason I came down the steps and here right before my eyes, she sat there. Unlike usual, I wanted to leap towards her and hug her. As the desire to do so blossomed, especially since Willie was still upstairs knocked out, I was ready to let go of every feeling felt and every feeling I had stupidly held onto at the funeral. At the moment, I was ready to become as many had been at the funeral. I wanted to release all that I knew was still inside of me. I wanted all of what I felt that was pressing against doors preventing their expansion to be felt, to be heard—just between me and her. Confirming to myself that if all this happened, even if Willie found his way coming down, I would hold nothing in. *I'm ready*, I thought to myself. But still, after thinking about being ready to do all this, within the split second following me turning around, I found myself unable to do any of what I was ready to do right then and there.

Though still on the floor, but after fully turning and seeing Mom, something else came with this comprehension of her being right there. It was a face and a look I had not seen before. The fear that her body portrayed did not have to be expressed by her scrunching up her body. It wasn't it making her teeth grind without any signs of rest. That was not how Mom expressed fear the few times I ever remembered her expressing it. Right now though, fear was stuck not on the face of Mom but deep into her dark quickly wavering pupils. Though still strong, Mom sat there trembling. As if waiting for the unwanted arrival of a presence, her eyes shot back and forth between me and what was behind me, as if looking through the blinds and further on through window. Her fear was obvious and struck my attention instantly after I turned. Though sitting there with a face gleaming from a previous sweat, Mom's quick and insecure facial expression caught my attention and she noticed it. She forced an empty and weak smile, but must have deep down known how blank it looked as the smile washed away without a single trace of previous existence.

"Are you okay," she asked, but it was nothing more than small talk to break the awkward silence yelling at both of us.

Both disregarding her question itself but still using it as the bridge I needed before beginning to ask for all that I felt I needed to know, "Mom, what happe-" I accidently began to shout.

Interrupting, "Alex," she began, but not before again grabbing my arm in a tough clinch with her left hand and sharply slapping her hand over my mouth with the other.

My eyes widened in a fear I felt that not only could be seen and noticed by her, but also matched to hers. Mom was never excessively physical towards me or Willie.

Dropping her head from the window and again towards me, both of the grips of her hands finally loosened. She started with a simple, "I don't know," but shortly after continued, "They are called Rebels.

They, well, so far, I mean. . ."

You're a wreck.

"Only one has been seen *here*. It's like the local news is keeping watch of a severe thunderstorm. I was paying attention to the news before I heard you get off the bed—the crick you made."

My heart sank far past my toes as Mom continued to tell me more than I wanted to know, but it was nothing less than she felt needed to be heard at this point.

"Do you think there are any more? Will more things like this continue to happen?"

"Alex," she started, but as she did, in direct response to the answer I anticipated soon to come, a cold chill flushed throughout my body. She noticed this and said no more before pulling me down towards her shoulder. I didn't have to say anything to her for her to know of the fear surging throughout and pounding in my head. She began to cry and soon after, I followed.

It hadn't even been a full 10 hours since Ms. Darlene's funeral. She was arguably the most important woman in our family's life and for the first time, we were there in the house without her. We were in her house without her. It didn't have to be said that this house would forevermore have an emptiness to it that could be felt miles away. The pain attached to this loss alone was enough to crumble even those who knew little of Ms. Darlene. This enormous amount of pain did not come alone. Almost hand-in-hand with this pain was that incomprehensible fear also introducing itself to us. Not only did I not know who to fear, but just as simply did not yet know what to fear.

"We don't care until it's at our front door knocking." It was like Mr. Hodge was sitting right there by me and Mom. I could almost see him with his back close to the corner of the wall and yet again exhaustedly saying it. Not looking towards us, instead his head tilted up analyzing the ceiling in the same way that Ms. Darlene would sometimes do during those nights that I then knew would never again come.

"We don't care. We don't. We-We don't care until it's at out front door knocking. Until it's at—knocking. Door knocking. We," I heard echoing continuously in my head as the words reached a ripple effect and began overlapping one another.

Mr. Hodge's words overlapped more and more wildly as they continued to grow louder. Mom's clinch wrapped tighter as if proclaiming then and there that I, no matter what, would not also be taken away from her. My sobs began dropping heavier until the alleviation from them left me feeling weightless. We remained there, her back against the wall and my head leaning on her, allowing sudden but brief waves of emotions to overtake and just as quickly depart from our bodies. No more words were said by either of us though we both remained awake. If nothing else, the constant ringing of sirens growing and fainting off in the near distance kept us awake and forcefully prevented me from forgetting or repressing the past 12 hours at that point.

I lay there involuntarily wondering if the sirens heard were travelling towards or away from instances involving these Rebels or if instead it was just like any other day on this side of town where sirens often rang like lullabies caressing the streets. The only thing reminding me of the amount of time that was passing was that slowly, the room grew from being dark to dim. It was one of those instances that you didn't notice until you finally and fully became aware of it

I fell asleep but woke shortly after. The dimness of the room had not left, but had only grew a few shades lighter. I looked up and saw that Mom was still awake. She wasn't wide awake, but still awake. Looking back at me, she smiled and gave me a kiss on my forehead. I felt I had long grown out of that being an acceptable thing between us, but at that moment, I comfortably smiled back towards her. Though asleep, and no longer with a soft smirk, Willie was sitting there on the other side of Mom with his head edged onto her shoulder in a sense that seemed to suggest that the weight of his big head was no longer bearable on his shoulders.

Again turning back and trading a smile with Mom, the three of us sat there. No words were said between us as the room continued to become less and less dim. It seemed that finally, sirens had discontinued their ringing. All that was left to do was to remain there, as the sun finally and fully shot through and then over the tree on the other side of the window, making its full presence known. As lovely as it was to see its beauty, I couldn't help but wonder to myself what it was that awaited us later in that day, and for days soon to come.

11

"I come from the Concrete Jungle," Mom randomly began breaking an evening silence.

The immediate days following Ms. Darlene's funeral and the city-wide scare mostly consisted of our guts being thoroughly and carefully wrenched. The silence filling the outside air was so profound that I had more of a chance hearing the thoughts of Mr. Hodge—dead or alive. The buzzing of the white noise quickly became unfamiliar. Sometimes within the hum were engines zooming from and to a destination somewhere in a distance. Especially because our house was in walking distance from I-640, even the random spurring of truck engines had not been heard for some time. While the frequency of them became rarer, even if an emergency vehicle—car or helicopter—was miles and miles away, they always seemed to come out of nowhere. Again though, though probably multiple miles away, because of the cautiously defined silence outside, it seemed like any emergency vehicle heard was right outside of the house as if there to rescue us.

One morning, the three of us there in the kitchen, Willie had got smacked so hard from Mom. Mom was carefully making us cereal. Randomly breaking the lingering silence that had seemed to have fully replaced Ms. Darlene and the empty feeling of her absence, Mom simply said in a voice just loud enough to not be considered a whisper, "It's a beautiful day outside."

Me and Willie, looked towards one another in confusion. Mom was standing at the counter smiling with a look of anticipation that could have waited hours for a response to come from either us.

"I thin—" I started but was quickly interrupted by Willie. I could only imagine what his charismatic self was going through. Initially, I didn't mind being interrupted because just as I was starting, I could see his face glow in a sense that had long been dulled-out. In fractions of time, his eyes widened, his smile stretched, and his aura began blooming as he shot up out of his seat.

"It is beautiful Mom—" he started to excitedly say. Before he could finish, only wanting to answer the question Mom just asked, pointing to the window with an over-extended arm that changed from him pointing to him reaching for the curtain. Just inches away from grabbing and pulling the curtain aside to add a visual emphasis to the answer he felt Mom should hear, Mom slapped him into a backwards stumble.

"Don't you touch," she started with yell, but quickly quieted to a fierce whisper, "or even dare to go towards that window, boy! Are you crazy?"

By this point we didn't know what had just happened. Before she continued and before I could rush over, almost ready to confront her, her eyes said to me all that was needed for me to understand. On one of Willie's dark cheeks, I couldn't tell whether or not I was actually seeing a red imprint left from Mom's swing.

"Listen here boy," she began as veins looked to be trying to escape the confinement of her arms and temples, "and you, too, Alex. None of us know what is outside these windows. Don't let me catch either of you moving towards this one or any of the windows of this house. You to understand me?"

It was a rhetorical question; not a moment after asking this question she had already stormed off upstairs and was not seen again until after the sun began setting. Right there, after Mom reached her room and closed the door, Willie stood motionless in the same spot Mom had smacked him back to. As much as I caught myself wanting to, I said and did nothing to her because I understood her. She was scared. She panicked. She was unsure what to do. She was extremely careful regarding the volumes of our voices. As much as she wanted to, she felt that if she screamed, that had just about as much potential to put us in a danger that none of us were yet familiar with. As a reflex, she smacked him and after she did, her eyes alone groaned from the agony she felt. She knew Willie didn't deserve it, but fully comprehending the possibility of who may have been outside watching, waiting, what had hurt her to do she decided was less painful than the hurt that could be felt had she not done anything. What could've happened if she allowed Willie to peek outside only to be met hand-in-hand with the presence of the worst case scenario? Slapping Willie hard enough to keep him getting to and moving the window blinds was the hardest safe decision.

Mom's closed door was not thick enough to prevent us from hearing the escaping quivers she failed to withhold. For a moment, I silently stood there behind Willie with both of my hands on his shoulders. For once I knew what to say to him. I knew how to comfort him as he stood there with both of his shoulders jerking up and down. Though for a moment, I could've sworn that I felt the same sting Willie had to have still been feeling, I quickly grew to appreciate the task Mom was able to do with complete effectiveness. He was, I was, she was, we were still safe. I wanted to explain to him that Mom only did that because of her fear for losing another loved one. Weirdly, more than anything, I found myself eager to explain to Willie my random epiphany that this, unlike anything else, was the epitome of "tough love."

"Willie, Mom is—"

"She didn't mean any hurt me did she, Alex?" Willie then turned facing me with the blankest stare. Before I could answer he responded, "I don't think she did. I was just stupid."

"Willie, you're not st—"

"It's okay, Alex. I love you," Willie hugged me and walked up to the room.

During the next few weeks, Willie never looked outside of the windows or even the peephole—as long as Mom was around at least. Aside from clocks, the easiness or difficulty of seeing objects close to you were the only signifiers that could give a relative estimate of the time of day.

"Have I ever told you about the Concrete Jungle," Mom asked one evening.

The storm outside was vicious and relaxing. It was the only one experienced during the immediate days following Ms. Darlene's funeral. Because of recent events, that alone made the storm unlike any of the storms that had ever found their way into our city. This storm in particular brought with it a certain grade of hail that made cracking sounds from hitting random windows when landing and instrumental tin-ringing tones from bouncing off many of the abandoned cars there along the streets of the neighborhood.

We were all laid out on the floor of the living room that night she began to tell. I'm sure at some point during the storm, as the intensity grew and showed no signs of even slightly slowing down, Mom started to think to herself that the Rebel or Rebels—who we hadn't heard anything more of since the funeral, which was at this point just under two weeks since—were surely not outside in this storm. Considering how peculiar she had been, that had to have been a thought that crossed Mom's mind and simmer a significant portion of the fear that was plaguing it.

Everything in the living room, had an inescapable grey-tint to it. No matter the vibrantly defined colors, the green, yellow, brown, and black—yes black—of the room, the sand-colored chair we still confirmed belonged to no one but Ms. Darlene, and the couches all had the tint. Whether belonging to the different plastic flowers or golden decorations stationed on each of the separate coffee tables or stands, and even the circular rug that stayed put in the middle of the room, they were all stripped of their vibrancies and now shared the same grey-tint; regardless of the sometimes surreal backgrounds speaking behind the bodies captured in the picture frames lined along the walls, or books that over time accumulated so much dust that they each looked about as old as the history many contained within their pages, every item and presence in the room, excluding one, had that same chilling melancholic tint that seemed to only become colder as the clapping of hail falling against the walls of the house became louder along with the booming of thunder and zinging of lightening acting only as an accent of the cacophony we were there on the floor listening to.

After she asked us this, I said nothing to Mom, but I guess my confused look of interest told her that I had no idea what this "Concrete Jungle" was. Swarms of butterflies began buzzing rampantly in my stomach. Before I realized it, I lost sight of everything by falling into a deep thought.

A Concrete Jungle? I heard a chuckle in my head. *This was it.* It was as clear as day. I thought it was something I could not pretend did not exist. I confirmed to myself that Mom had finally lost it. I patiently waited for days for when the "make it or break it" moment would come for her and with her asking this, I knew the time had finally arrived. My purpose for life, no longer partial, had finally and fully activated. Mom, speaking and acting as she did ever since the funeral, bit by bit was progressively losing it. I felt that my responsibility for the upbringing and becoming the provider for Willie was here.

I had long told myself that I was to be such for Willie and strived to prepare myself for whenever the day would come. Careful mental preparation and training seemed to have been for nothing because right there, next to Mom and Willie, hearing myself tell myself that it was time, I felt a weakness never before felt. *I'm not ready.*

Fail.

"Are you OK, Alex?" I heard also feeling a nudge. The nudge was a savior that snapped me out of a painful realization that had unnoticeably blackened my vision. After that nudge, I was back there on the floor, hearing the storm, and right there directly seeing the one thing that the grey tint hadn't consumed.

That look behind Mom's eyes was all that I needed then. While supposedly confirming that it was finally time for me to step up, the sudden realization that I wasn't ready quickly, effortlessly became unavoidably acknowledged by me. From the nudge and the question, I saw a familiar look that hadn't been seen for a while. When I made eye contact with Mom, I noticed that there was not a single presence of a grey-tint to her. She wasn't vibrant or anything close to being such, but still, unlike ever before since the funeral, again, I was looking at the Mom I remembered. Finally. The Mom that was there with me and Willie, during the storm, was giving a similar intimate look Ms. Darlene shared to any and all that she made eye contact with. But still, right then, Mom was giving me a look that alone confirmed, "I have something I need you to hear while I'm here able to tell you."

Before beginning to tell me aspects of her life she had never told me and surely not Willie, she looked over to him. As usual, Willie was absent from all consciousness. Slobber trickling down his wide-opened mouth, he looked nothing less than a baby bird calling for momma bird to bring dinner. I think that we were sharing the same thoughts. After taking notice of Willie and then looking back up to Mom, we both smiled, surely separately but simultaneously thinking, "I'd be crazy to expect anything less from you, Willie."

As Mom began to speak, if I were to close my eyes right then, I would've imagined that nothing recent had happened. What was being felt right then had a familiarity to it. The growing intimacy felt between us at that moment was the same felt with Ms. Darlene. Understand that it was to the extent that I actually wondered if I were to look over towards Ms. Darlene's chair now, would she be right there with us leaning back and looking towards the ceiling as she always did throughout weekday evenings. The only difference between that instance of me and Mom and the ones between me and Ms. Darlene was reality. That the chair was empty and would remain as such, and unlike the many occasions between me and Ms. Darlene, Mom was only able to tell me of her past this one time.

"I always considered myself a product of the 'Concrete Jungle.' While I always lived in East Knoxville, thanks to Ms. Darlene, we now live in what many would proclaim as the 'safer' portion of the East Knoxville area. But growing up, I lived in the district of East Knoxville where I, and the majority of others of the area, were seen as being just a little more than animals, not quite acknowledged as fellow humans to several in Knoxville, Tennessee."

Never had I felt so close to Mom. People seemed to *always* expect the worst from East Knoxville. There were times when after hearing that I was from East Knoxville, whether on a field trip shared between schools or just out with Willie at the mall, kids my age and some even older asked crazy questions that alone showed what they thought and felt of our community.

"I heard a teacher shot a student," one random boy said in a questioning way and then waited, looking at me or Willie for some kind

of confirmation. While I felt a heat of infuriation, Willie simultaneously and easily told the boy that no such thing had happened and
laughed like it was the best joke he had heard in a while. I felt it was
nothing to laugh at. It was insulting. I never told her of this or any
other situations like this, but considering what Mom had just said, I
wish I would've told her of the many times people had said these
things to us. I saw then that after all this time, she would've known
exactly how to respond and comfort—as if she wouldn't have been
able to do such regardless.

"It wasn't always just because we were black," Mom stated. As she
spoke, it was as if outside the window was a script she was reading
from; lying down on her lap and looking up to her, I saw that as she
spoke, her eyes were travelling from far side to side. In between every
shift, she was transferring from word to word, memory to memory.
By this time, there was no hint of containment within Mom's voice.
Despite, for days, Mom's refusal to speak anything louder than a
murmur, she now spoke as though it was impossible to further
withhold explaining what she now felt was the perfect time to
share—reality. The consistent subtleness and the anxiety that was
buried deep within her whispering was a painful reminder ready to
slap us if there was even the slightest sign of forgetting anything
recent, but during the slow passing of the storm that evening, as she
began speaking and telling me of this "Concrete Jungle," no hint of
any previous distress was present.

"While of course being black contributed to the lack of humanity
I saw in the eyes of some when focusing on me," she continued, "it
was just one factor of many others that contributed to this image.
Simply, it was where I was from that had a capability of devolving
me from human standards. Alex, as it sort of is today, growing up,
despite the image of East Knoxville, there actually was a sort of
plethora of demographics within this side of the city. Growing up,
me and some of my friends would always meet up and walk down a

few blocks to one of the gas stations down Magnolia. No matter if we went during the peak of the summer heat or after the 6pm sunset of a winter evening, no matter if black, white, purple, or blue, males or females, devout Christian, Atheist, or Muslim, regardless which demographic you belonged to, for many it didn't matter if seen in East Knoxville. All that was seen by most of the remainder of Knoxville was that you were from East Knoxville. Sometimes, all because of different placements in the same city, the same look of disgust was sometimes even in the eyes of those you could share a demographic with."

I was caught in thought again. We sat at just the right angle to barely be able to see up under the window blinds. Flashes of lightening allowed me to see, for just a moment, the leaves of the trees scrimmaging along branches beneath a quickly darkening night. Out of the corner of my eyes, I could only see Mom's mouth moving. I swear this was one of the things I always struggled most with. Only sometimes did people ask about things they heard about East Knoxville. Regardless of the plausibility of whatever it was that they may have heard, more often than not, I was *told*, by someone from another side of town, what it was surrounding *me*. I never lied to myself about some of the problems we faced in East Knoxville. There were struggles I took notice of. Still, while not even a quarter of a fraction as rough as some places in the state, let alone the nation, East Knoxville was still the Concrete Jungle, as Mom had put it, and in the eyes of some, we were of the "Land of Nightmares."

In East Knoxville, because of the myths that were alone the molders of the image people had of this area, I remember the struggle me and Willie had getting home the same night that boy told us about what he'd heard of the teacher shooting a student. After finally leaving him and walking around the mall, before we knew it, it was time for the mall to close. Walking outside, it was always easy to locate taxis. Mom had already given us money to get back home because by the time she knew we wanted to leave the mall, she would still be at work and Ms. Darlene would've been several hours into a deep sleep. Getting to the only taxi left, it was then that we learned that after a certain time, some taxi owners, like the one that night, regardless of business and despite the extra money we were willing to give him, refused all fares to or from East Knoxville. As weird as it was for me, a policeman volunteered to drop us off at home that night.

A pounding felt from thunder snapped me back to listening to Mom. The sun was basically gone. Mom was still speaking. She hadn't noticed my day-dreaming—that or she didn't care.

After, for a period following Mom's speaking, we sat in a complete darkness only able to be escaped from with the help of the lightening slitting through the room but then also leaving us temporarily blind. The storm did all but quiet down. Rain and hail no longer fell but were instead thrown from the clouds.

We silently sat there listening to the music banging outside. Noticing Mom chuckle after turning from her right shoulder, it was then that I realized how deeply captivated I had been during the passing of the night. Looking to where she had just turned away from, wanting to share the same chuckle, Willie somehow found his way to the center of the room looking like fresh roadkill. Due to how high and low his stomach was becoming, along with his tongue halfway hanging from a dropped jaw, I could tell that he was savagely snoring. Amazingly, he seemed nothing more than a channel that was muted at the request of the storm's desire to further be heard.

I felt that it was my turn to break the silence and do my part in contributing to the conversation being had between Mom and me. It was then that I realized we had stopped being cautious. Unlike Willie, as though she were in a direct combat against the consistent booming brought on by the tireless storm, Mom found herself fearlessly yelling in an excessive effort to be heard. She was winning. On the other hand, when I spoke, I almost had to plug my own ears to better hear myself and ensure that I was saying only what I was thinking.

Regardless, giving a little more effort to being better heard, I decided to tell Mom the resulting thoughts coming from the repeating of her recent words in my head. What I told her were thoughts I always wanted to express, but felt too insecure to tell anyone. Even Ms. Darlene.

"What is worse about being *seen* as products from this 'Concrete Jungle,' as you call it Mom, is that sometimes, some can't help but finally become these products they are seen as. How does a girl know she is beautiful if she is often told that she is homely, or if she is just never told that she is beautiful at all? It's obviously harder for her to know she has the potential of being a Queen just as it is harder for a boy to know his potential of being no less of a King than any other if he and she are looked upon and treated as just simpletons."

"How do you see yourself, dear?"

Truth be told, I knew what she wanted to hear right then. I knew what I wanted to hear myself say to her in response, but I felt it would've taken away from what was being felt. Honestly to me, Willie was always the Prince soon to be a King. I sometimes barely felt qualified of being related to him. When I recently mentioned to her the potential of boys and girls being seen as royalty, I purposefully used "potential". I always felt that one of the honest truths to the world's existence was that not everyone could be Kings and Queens. If such was the case, if all were able to become one of the two, what would then be the power and beauty behind being considered and seen as one? With having long since felt I wasn't one, this, in result, always made me even happier to see and consider Willie as one of the few potentials.

Finding a way to successfully avoid answering Mom's question, I told her something I always felt, but never told to her.

"Mom, we're blessed to have you." As I said this, her soft embrace grew firmer. Before I knew it, further explanation began revealing itself.

"We had two Queens raising us. We were blessed to have not one but two individuals I've always seen as royalty. Some, regardless of having both parents or not, don't have any royalty."

I found myself almost out of breath and with a tingling feeling from the passion I was feeling that night. Before I could continue from the brief pause I took, Mom spoke saying, "And because of this, Alex, several of the diamonds and jewels within the minds of many from East Knoxville are only covered with a little dirt, and because of some of the dirt on them, sometimes coming even from their own eyes when they see their reflections, many jewels then mistaken as the same crap that could be easily found in someone's yard. This learned helplessness molds people into believing that they are a specific brand of crap that doesn't have the luxury of even coming from a homeless mutt."

As Mom said this, it was as though she were no longer fighting against the storm that still hadn't quieted in the slightest bit. As she spoke, she and the storm seemed to be working alongside each other. As Mom continued, at coinciding moments, thunder and lightning accented whatever it was she was saying with their arrivals and departures. The longer Mom spoke, the easier it was to notice that her energy became one with the storm. Just as Mom finally began to slow down the speed of her speaking and lower the volume of her words, so, too, did the sound and fierceness of the storm dwindle.

The last thing Mom expressed before beginning to bridge us into another period of complete silence was, "Ms. Darlene took us in when I was 22, you were about four years old and I was pregnant with Willie. While it was only supposed to be temporary, my pride suggesting that I was ready for us to live on our own far before actually being able to, Ms. Darlene would not hear it, and refused to let us leave."

I felt a flush of sadness. With Mom saying this, I thought back to the picture of all of us standing together. Not that I wasn't any longer missing her, but the forced coping I found myself able to forge vanished and I felt myself missing her all over again.

"When the time came that I was actually ready for us to leave out this house and live out on our own, Ms. Darlene grew severely ill. She could no longer work. It was without question that I told her that I wouldn't leave her by herself. It was so quick that I saw her as a mother to me and a grandmother to you two, Alex. And so it remains.

"Alex, Ms. Darlene and I have long and will forever remain proud of you. I had a dream that she was in heaven looking down with the biggest smile directed specifically to you as she often had as she lived. W-we often talked about how wise you were and you still are. You are one of a kind, dear."

By this point, though not heavily, I felt droplets falling from above onto my cheeks as she continued, "I'm not sure what the future holds, Alex. I just wish—" Though she tried several times to finish whatever it was she wanted to tell me, at this point, she couldn't. Deep sniffling prevented her every time she tried to begin until she ceased and complied by just sitting there with me and listening to the silence.

"I love you, Alex," Mom suddenly and quickly said while rubbing the side of my head.

This was something rarely said, but often felt. Because it wasn't said often, there was also an awkward feeling felt every one of the few times it was said by Mom. I never told her, but I wish it was said more often. I didn't like that it was a feeling of awkwardness the times the phrase was finally said. I felt if it was said more often, then that would eliminate the feeling, but I always, maybe selfishly felt that it shouldn't be me to say it first. Willie always said it though—to both of us. The times she would say it to both of us at the same time, almost before mom could finish, Willie would respond for the both of us with saying, "*We* love you, too," on his behalf as well as mine. Willie always doing this, I often only nodded as a sort of confirmation that I approved of him saying this on my behalf.

For whatever reason, I panicked. A short time had passed but no response was given. Mom had noticed. She knew I was awake from having heard me picking the skin on sides of my thumbs for some time now. Just after Mom said this, I froze with taking in a deep breath. Her rubbing the side of my head stopped as well. Unlike ever before, I could feel that right then she deeply wanted, needed to hear me say it back to her.

"I love you, too, Mom," I said, but without wanting to. But that was ok. I needed to. I didn't want to say it only out of stupid insecurities. A deep exhale came from Mom and the rubbing of the side of my head continued. Unable to see anything now, as the storm was gone to the extent that even rain discontinued to fall, soft thunders were still heard off beyond in some distance. If nothing else, I knew Mom was there with me smiling and would continue smiling as long as we remained on the living room floor. Before passing out, I could only hope that she knew that I was smiling, too.

12

The night continued to pass. The storm never returned. Silence remained. All of this, but I couldn't stay asleep. Every time I came close, it felt like I was pinched in my arm and purposefully forced to wake up. Then back to being far from dozing off, I would look around. Every time, Mom still remained there, head against the wall and lifted in what looked to be a comfortable sleep. Willie, on the other hand, though still in an unbreakable sleep, always moved at least six times after somewhere close to three minutes of stillness.

It was a cycle. After several times in, taking notice of the same things, I decided to screw trying and just stay awake. *Fail.* At the moment, I had no intentions of even moving from the comfort my body had found. The last time I woke, I was on my back with my neck and the back of my head perfectly molded along Mom's upper thigh.

If I tilted my head up just a little, still within the newfound comfort-zone, I was able to take notice of that same Mom that would take time to get reacquainted with. About three weeks since the funeral, because of the scare, still unsure of what was on the other side of the door, across the lawn, and down what could've been just blocks over, Mom chose not to return to any of her jobs. For her, work, though obviously necessary, was overly draining; before all of this, during those school nights as well as those past summers, she usually enforced bedtimes. During a majority of those past nights, for years, with Willie long asleep and me usually not asleep but still lying down, the majority of my interaction with Mom consisted of her closing the front door deep into the night after finally coming home and me hearing a temporary humming of the living room TV being turned on. That was if and only if something had happened to make her want to watch the 11pm local news.

Not including times where she may have only had two jobs instead of three—though most likely she was already looking for a third—the few moments me or Willie were able to briefly speak to her only included us coming home just before she left for her last job, or her refusal to miss a school's ceremony celebrating an achievement of mine or Willie's. During those brief moments of our interaction in the past, a degree of tiredness was almost always visibly stationed under and within her eyes. Regarding her inescapable irritableness, she acknowledged it and tried to hide it, but often couldn't.

This was the Mom I grew up seeing, but right there in front of me, head tilted upward and fast asleep was the Mom Ms. Darlene often reminded me about. In this darkness, I could see a vibrancy that was often overshadowed, but still always present. Mom always smiled, but this, what I was seeing as the night continued to creep along, had warmth, comfort, and exemplified the compassion Ms. Darlene constantly stressed was always present.

As if she could see me through her eyelids, I returned to her a delicate smile. When my head wasn't tilted up on Mom's thigh, I would instead look slightly downwards. The living room window was right there. Though the white-based, light green floral patterned curtains were stretched over the blinds and the window, I was still able to clearly see through them as if nothing at all was there. It was because at one point during the night, the now puny moon had been distinctly looking at me. I thought to myself that the moon was looking for me in hopes that I could give the remainder of it to make it again whole. Regardless of not even being a quarter of a whole moon, there was still a significant brightness provided by it.

While unmistakably gorgeous, the moon irritated me. I allowed myself to become envious. Right then, I could clearly see all that I had been deprived of being around for what seemed like years following years. Since waking up in the house after the funeral, I had not stepped a single foot outside. The few times I took a chance and looked beyond the curtains and blinds to speedily take notice of all that I could, those moments were way too brief to suffice my hunger for more. When the opportunity presented itself, when she would go to use the bathroom, wash-up and change clothes, or walk down the hall to decide which of our non-perishable foods would be the small meal of the day, desperately, I starved to look out and see all that I could while unavoidably also overlooking several aspects of the outside view; I needed to do so before Mom came back to whichever room of the house we were all in at that moment. It was risky because sometimes, as me and Willie soon learned, we did not know how long Mom would be gone.

For example, "I'm not feeling good," Mom had claimed one previous evening.

Personally, I was confused because shortly before saying this, she showed absolutely no sign of any discomfort being present. She looked anxious. Out of nowhere, she bent over, arms wrapped her stomach, and was slightly pushing back and forth.

"Are you okay, Mom?" Willie asked halfway petrified.

"I think it was just something I ate. I have to use the bathroom. I'll be right back," she stated already leaving the kitchen.

Though he was genuinely frightened by the sudden pain Mom claimed she was in, the second Mom turned the corner to walk to the bathroom, Willie turned towards me with a wide smile. His nod told me what was now on his mind. He was at the window before I was able to cast off my concern for Mom. There he stood. He stood there as if on the other side of it was every one of his favorite candies and foods. His face was no more than centimeters away from the glass—if not completely one with it.

It happened just as suddenly as the first time it happened. Before Willie could comprehend the deep lunges of steps that were coming towards him, and before I even saw her coming back around the corner of the wall, Mom's hand had seemed to have long since connected and departed from his face.

"I told you not to do that," was all she said and was all that would be said until she told us to come upstairs because it was time for us to do our wash-ups. But between the times leading up to her finally saying this and the time following him getting slapped for the second time, Willie did not cry nor did I walk to comfort him.

What Willie didn't know was that I envied him. There on Mom and admiring the thin revealing of beauty I was able to see through the narrow window slightly covered by a thinly designed curtain and sloped blinds, I still was unable to see all that Willie refused to go without seeing. Though, without question, she was asleep, and it would have been pretty easy for me to near soundlessly crawl towards the window to see even more, I wouldn't allow myself to do such. To cover up the fear I had of being caught, several times I told myself that night that it was simply not worth it. And so I saw only what that angle of the window allowed for me to see of the moon shining down on the streets below.

It wasn't until much later that I realized there was a third area I could focus on without having to move out of my comfortable position on Mom. Time continued to pass and it finally reached a point that the room was no longer pitch dark. It wasn't because my eyes had adjusted to the dark, which they had, but because so much time had passed since I decided to stay awake. Daylight, though not quite here, was just a number of breaths away.

Finally succumbing to the desire and thus studying, seeing only the little bit but still all that I could, through the thin spaces between the blinds, outside, the pitch of darkness had now been replaced with the slow resurfacing of a sun that couldn't have been but a few miles under the horizon far off. The moon had long departed, but the gleaming of everything it shined on was still sparkling from the wetness the storm had left as a present. Everything had a dark grey, navy blue tint accentuating its visibility. Eventually, the tint able to only be seen outside, unnoticeably found its way inside. The gradual brightening of things was so slow but progressive

At one point, as the transition from night to day continued to tiptoe, between looking from Mom back down to the window, there just below Mom's chin but not yet at the window, I was caught by the corner of the living room. Though nothing more than a simple corner, instantly, looking and seeing nothing, my mind began to work. This became the last focus point. Stuck now looking deep into the corner, I began seeing memories. What was crazy was the fact that, for a second, I had complete control over which of my memories were able to be seen.

That corner basically provided a stretched-out screen for memories to be vividly displayed. The appreciation and luxury I found there waiting in that corner was as shortly lived as the time it took for me to make a soon to come abrasive decision.

As if preprogrammed on an established timer, captivated by what was coming and going, again, though looking into what was nothing more than a corner, images and thoughts continued to be seen. Different thoughts were coming and leaving so quickly that I didn't always have enough time to fully comprehend what was just displayed. The thoughts seemed to have no sense of connection to the ones seen before nor the ones that would come directly after. Some of the blitzing thoughts were significant while others contained things I hadn't thought of since whatever thought being displayed actually happened.

At one point, coming from the nothingness that was there at the smallest point of the corner, just as every thought did, expanding with a swiftness until able to fully be seen, I saw Willie being tickled by Mom on what was his sixth birthday. I could almost feel the sensation of joy that was there in the screams coming from him asking Mom to stop though all of us knew he meant the opposite. Gone. The memory never quit expanding until nothing more was able to be seen from it, but just as that was happening, I would take notice of another quickly approaching from the same small point of the corner until it, whatever it contained, expanded beyond further existence.

There came a memory of a janitor unlocking the school doors one morning before she was supposed to. It was nice of her because that morning it was raining hard. Only a few of us outside had an umbrella. Though I had a big one, only a few kids were able to come share it with me. Gone. Then came another one just as suddenly as the umbrella memory had left. This one had me watching a faint memory containing a time that was just before Willie was born. Mom was there on the couch. In this memory she looked to be caught in the process of imploding. She was humungous!

"Your little brother is almost here, sweetie," she said to me.

Gone. Faded. Leaving as another came. The most interesting thing I finally took realization of as I continued to watch these random memories come and go was the fact that some, while they were definitely my memories, I wasn't always watching and seeing them through my eyes.

The second time Willie had gotten smacked for peaking outside of the window was one of the memories coming out of the nothingness of the corner. I wasn't seeing that memory through anyone's eyes because as the memory became fully visible, I saw Willie, I saw Mom, and I also saw myself. I was viewing the scene as an outsider—in third person. The focus of this memory briefly shifted to the look I had after Mom had smacked him. I remembered the feeling I had after it had happened, but I had no idea how pathetic I had looked. If this memory was a scene of a movie that I had just randomly walked in on at a theater, if it weren't for the faint imprint left on Willie's face, I would've just as easily guessed that I was the one who had been smacked. That was how pitiful I looked. Gone.

I wasn't always sure how to take the few memories that were like this. I didn't always have time to fully take in the display I was seeing before it left. Coming, I saw what I think was Chimney Top Mountains just after a rain shower. Gone. Coming, I noticed the view of one of the gas stations on Magnolia while it snowed. Gone. Memories of Mr. Hodge, McDonalds, a house on fire, watching a flood washing over and through a city in India, seeing 9/11 coverage during school, holding hands with Willie and Mom during a concert downtown, and tears falling from my face were all some of the memories sprinting towards and away from my view. Then it came.

"Ms. Darlene!" I shot up from Mom's lap.

This one had come just as quickly as the others, but unlike them, it stayed without any signs of leaving. Unlike the previous ones, as this one began to expand towards my view, I was able to comprehend this one far quicker than the others. For a second, as I began understanding what this one in particular contained, I initially wished it was one of the ones that came and went before I was able to grasp what it contained. On the contrary, this one had an incomparable vividness to it. "Ms. Darlene," I said while acknowledging how much this sighting of her reminded me that I missed her.

With all the will power I had, I had tried not to think much of her since her funeral because of the obvious pain any memory of her never failed to bring with it, to me, even when triggered by the slightest and simplest reminders. Seeing her chair, smelling a specific scent in the house, and seeing her favorite pair of slippers that she never forgot to change into when she came into the living room were each of the many triggers I tried to avoid making the smallest form of contact with. Surprisingly, with time, the suppression of remembering her began to succeed. So quickly had all of that effort instantly become worthless as her image, in that same corner, continued to grow closer to me.

As Ms. Darlene came closer, all over again, I saw a specific beauty that only could belong to her. Focusing specifically on her, in this image, she was standing upright with hands cuffed in front of her pelvic area in a humble but still welcoming manner. Her dress was a simple green, but was perfectly accented in bright golden jewelry—just like much of the living room. For someone who may not have known her, pertaining to this view I was seeing of her, she could've easily been mistaken as an empress of some country abroad. Finally close enough in view, all over again, I took notice of my favorite aspect of her—her smile. Though showing no teeth, her smile right then remained as serene as it always was. It was just like one of those mornings before me and Willie left for school and no less as peaceful as I remember it being before they finally closed her casket.

By then, while I felt refreshed at contentedly welcoming a memory I had avoided, I found myself ready for the memory to pass and began to purposefully try and search through Ms. Darlene. I was ready to see what the next memory would provide for me, but not only did nothing come from the small point of the corner that every other memory started and expanded from, when I unfocused on the corner, Ms. Darlene still remained there standing in the same humble and welcoming way dressed in the same seemingly idol-like attire.

Eye contact was established. I was extremely focused on the eye contact made, because at first, I looked into the center of her pupils to see if the view of her was expanding in even the least bit. No. The eye contact was snapped in half when she began fully turning her head, looking around her while suggesting that I do the same. I wasn't sure if her surroundings in this display came out of nowhere or if it was always there, but simply seeing her made me neglect anything that was not her.

Regardless, as I began seeing what she was looking at, I was there all over again. We were there at her funeral. It at the point of the chaos following the several rings and vibrations of phones that signaled the beginning that led to where we now were. All over again, I heard screams, felt the waves of fear pushing over. Hoping to break this vision, I closed my eyes so that I would no longer see the corner and what it and Ms. Darlene was forcing me to see, but closing them did nothing. The difference between my eyes being open and shut was so minimal that I could barely tell one from the other. Trapped.

The only difference between being at the funeral and this memory of it was that just like the coming and going of some of the other memories, I wasn't seeing this one in first person. Following Ms. Darlene, she walked as if none of the chaos was happening around her, and though no longer smiling, but not at all frowning, she stopped and stood right there behind me, right there in this vision.

Was this what I looked like?

Moving only when pushed by people running and bumping into me, eyes big and wide but still dull and bare, I looked no more alive than was Ms. Darlene during all of this. Finally, while looking square in the eyes of the me that was re-watching all of this—the actual me—she slowly bent down and placed both of her hands on the shoulders of me in the memory. Moving no more than I was already,

I remained still and stagnant, but as I watched this, I jerked from the rush of chills because as I saw her hands grip, I swear it felt like I could feel her placing her hands on the me that was watching this in the living room. I looked up, but she wasn't there. Still, I felt her hands. The sensation I felt of her grip tightening made me look back at her in the corner.

Slowly tilting her head towards my ears but with eyes refusing to break contact with me as I watched, I saw her mouth move, and as her lips moved I heard, "bury me." The view of the entire vision quickly shifted over to her casket that was now turned sideways on the ground of the sanctuary just as I last saw it. Before seeing anything more, the view of the casket was the final sight of this memory before it expanded out of existence.

Eyes shooting open, before I could fully comprehend and take in all that I had seen, I was already down past the yard in the middle of the street, my running fueled by raw intuition.

13

The hell are you doing, Alex?
  "Yes," was all I could manage to say in response to blaring thoughts.

It was no later than 6 in the morning. Though it may have been in the upper 60's of this early June morning, the clouds covering any hint of the specific location of the sun, the moistness that was still yet to be picked up from Nature's war the previous night, and the consistent streaming push of wind against my body made it feel like a mid-November night. Everything I saw and everything I felt as I ran had a melancholic essence to it. The morning being an overcast one didn't help. It continued slowly becoming brighter, but with this, it still remained no less silver than the world's most valuable sword. Aside from battling every doubt and question being thrown around my head regarding how stupid I was currently feeling, the gloom of the morning was a whole different battle being fought as I ran.

The gloom was what I would imagine hearing in the whisper of a smiling sadistic criminal that was lurking behind and telling me everything was going to be all right with a knife in hand, up to your neck and the other arm wrapped around your chest. No escape. It was the feeling that there was an unavoidable future that could be fought against—delayed—but remained impossibly avoidable.

Do you feel that?

I was barefoot. While I was running in light-blue gym shorts, a plain crimson red shirt, my dreadlocks pulled all the way back but still flapping and bouncing with individual launch, I was still trying to catch up to the reflexive thoughts that involuntarily sent me running out of the house without considering a single response, effect, consequence, or outcome of my action.

What if they are out there?

What if Mom wakes up, doesn't see you, and leaves the house looking for you and is seen by them?

Do you even know a thing about who this "they" and "them" are?

Do you first know where you are going and how to get there?

Willie.

I was hearing each of these thoughts and more. Each came from different voices, and with the different voices, a different feeling emphasized whatever the thought said or questioned. Some of the thoughts were louder than the others. Some were fearful, some ridiculed and mocked me. Each thought followed the other with little space in between—sometimes overlapping with no space. Every thought heard had with it an addition of weight I had no choice but to carry with me. Each one felt like an extra rubber band wrapped around me and the house; stretching these bands became harder. The feeling of doubt, continued growing louder. By this point, it was too late to turn around. My only choice was to continue running until some of the pulling rubber bands broke.

What was that!? Over there?

Paranoia had never been so strong. As I ran, while I wasn't ready for that time to come, I knew that at any moment *this could be it; right now; in a second; one more step.* My eyes quickly learned to go in all directions. I swear I could see straight through and around the houses and buildings on the blocks I was passing. It felt as though I was almost able to see things that were just outside of my vision as if they were there in front of me. What was even worse was the eerie feeling I felt from not knowing if I heard something out there or if it was my mind playing sick tricks on me.

While I didn't really know what a ground-zero warzone would look like, this area of East Knoxville still looked like it was close enough to wherever ground-zero was to still be affected by the events of it. Some gas stations were stocked with cars left abandoned while other cars were abandoned completely in the middle of the streets. Along with the windows of several other houses and businesses, I took specific notice of a city-renowned pawn shop's window completely busted from looters that left only simple items of inventory behind. In different lawns and along the sides of streets, I saw bikes. There was a tricycle that was there completely crumpled. Seeing this, for a just second as I continued to sprint pass the tricycle, I imagined that just before the shock of fear completely consumed the city, there was some kid, maybe a young girl, riding that pink tricycle. All she was doing was enjoying pedaling up and down East 5th Ave. Before being able to comprehend what had just happened, and before being able to be saved by a mom or dad running out of house to find and pick her up, the last thing this little girl saw and heard, before fear was able to make its presence known to her, was the bumper of a screeching car unable to stop in time.

Unlike ever before, everything I was seeing looked like a Season 1 scene from *The Walking Dead.* As I ran down the street, despite the fact that it was morning, not only did I not see anyone, I heard no sound from anyone or anything. By this time of the day, even when

9/11 had happened, Magnolia still had its flurry of business and cars zooming up and down the street. Now, nothing. Not only was there a chilling absence of moving cars, I took notice that for days now, there hadn't even been a single siren of any emergency vehicle singing its melody like the perception of the Concrete Jungle would suggest.

Finally it fits in, one truthful but nevertheless random thought felt it was necessary to remind me.

Seeing the rapidly becoming decrepit remains of East Knoxville, I thought of the "The Odd Fellows' Cemetery." This cemetery was the most valuable piece of trash. Trash only because of the way people chose to look at it. It was treated and seen as trash despite the history within its grounds.

"The first black millionaire in Knoxville, Calvin 'Cal' Johnson, is buried in the Odd Fellows' cemetery," Mr. Hodge sometimes saw fit to remind the class. "Mr. Cal Johnson as well as Mr. William Yardley, a man who had enough courage to become a candidate for governor of Tennessee."

While these were two of the ones he admired most, from being mentioned *every time* he spoke of the cemetery, Mr. Hodge often saw fit to tell us about a number of the others also buried within these grounds, covered by "shrouds of disrespect," as both Mr. Hodge and Ms. Darlene, at different times, identically claimed.

It was only recently that groups and organizations began a campaign to reconstruct and return the beauty that many felt the cemetery was deprived of. Within the neighboring graveyards of East Knoxville, and especially the ones throughout the city, it was easy to sometimes take notice of the most vibrant roses and flowers that always seemed to be personally chosen to decorate the tombstones of loved ones, or simply those belonging to people and figures of the city that many felt deserved respect—whether soldiers, doctors, teachers, etc. While this was the case for, I'm sure, the majority of graveyards throughout Knoxville, it wasn't always so at the Odd Fellows' Cemetery.

At one point, as if a carefully chosen replacement for flowers to be laid across tombstones or replacements for the grass of the graveyard in general, empty 40 ounce bottles of malt liquor, sometimes shattered from being tossed out of cars in passing, provided a specific dirty-stained gleam where the sun couldn't help but shine down on the cemetery. Empty orange-tinted prescription pill bottles, torn cigarette boxes, abandoned fast-food containers, or the broken tombstones knocked over *not* by any storms or the fallen tree branches that remained on the grounds for what seemed like years at a time, but instead by the sometimes randomly drunken creeping throughout the cemetery during the height of weekday nights by those who, in a sense, looked as though they were trying to locate their personal burial grounds. *This* was how I imagined East Knoxville's Odd Fellows' Cemetery to be whenever I talked about it.

Finally, though, this image of the cemetery fit within all that I was able to take notice of as I continued storming down the streets. With some of the burnt-to-the ground households I saw, shattered street lights, cable lines looking like wimpy cousins of stalactites, and then the number of tossed-aside trash cans with holes from caved-in dents that I saw, this Concrete Jungle Mom had told me of looked as if it actually came from something unavoidable instead of being a product of neglect and deprivation or a checkpoint reached as a part of a scheme for a later, coming Knoxville.

There was only one thing providing a small ounce of comfort. Though they couldn't be directly seen, I still knew they were there sitting on the branches of coming and passing trees that stood and remained looking almost completely unaffected by any of the recent events. The birds sat there and the birds sang. Though I couldn't tell how many different types of birds, I knew that there were enough present to give the song I was hearing the necessary different parts to create a masterpiece. As tired as I was, this song I was hearing was nothing less than having a song with the powerful bass and quick tempo needed for a runner to tap into that second wind that my gym teacher always mentioned.

The farther I ran, it seemed the louder the birds sang. Nothing else was present. I no longer felt or heard the different constraints of thoughts, but I barely held on to what it was I was doing or where it was I was heading. Joining the song being heard, I felt the beating of my heart bumping as if refusing to be outdone. Out of nowhere, a competition was made. The longer it was that I continued to run the fiercer the competition became. At one point it was my heart that became the tempo holder speeding up the song from where it previously was. Then louder and stronger, the individual birds strived and succeeded to even further speed up the rhythm as the new self-asserted tempo holders. Every climax reached was again to be out-climaxed. Seeing nothing around me now, still running and paying attention to the battle of tempo holders, the singing of birds and the pounding of my heart, I finally reached a point, a speed, to where the song and tempo could not be distinguished from one another. Before I realized it, it became a simple vibration that caused me to become numb to the world.

Just as it was when I first left the house, it remained that I was running and doing without being in control. I was now in a sort of auto-pilot and in my mind, I fell into an abyss; I was seeing nothing, feeling only the thrust of individual leaps taken, hearing nothing more than a buzzing. I remained in this state of being, running where intuition took me.

Pulled once again from the darkness and back into reality, I saw again. It all slowed until again I heard the definite song sung by the birds. I deemed my pulse as the victor of the competition because the attractive chirping of several birds could again be heard and distinguished from one another, but my heart felt as though it had the energy to beat on for hours to come. I found myself on my knees and out of breath. The weight once felt from the pressuring thoughts felt multiplied. Sweat was dripping between my fingers which were crinkling from the profound support they were not prepared to provide. Gasps for air felt counterproductive. Every inhale came with the feeling of being punched by the most precise boxer; every following exhale felt like a purposeful straining of my lungs, but still, above, I could hear an ongoing masterpiece.

It took what felt like hours for me to even in the slightest bit regain composure. Gaining enough strength to finally lift my head from my elbows, transferring the support of my weight solely to knees dug deep into the soil of a front lawn, despite exhaustion still present, I took notice that I was finally there.

"College Hille Church," there barely able to be read on the front banner.

The church fit in well. Just as it was regarding all that I saw as I ran to the church, the church looked like everything else and everything I knew it would look like as we were leaving from the interrupted funeral. Things here were more congested though. There was no way for a car to come into the parking lot of the church. At every one of the three entrances of the whole parking lot, a closed-in collision of three or so prevented any entering and exiting of the parking lot by means of any vehicle.

The doors of the church were wide open. Though nowhere near as fast as it was while coming, but still fiercely, my heart all but continuously imploded on itself.

What if they are in there?

I found myself chuckle at this thought after noticing the fear it was mumbled with. If there was anyone inside the church, if it was someone who was a part of the Rebellion, it was simple, that was it. If they saw and decided to chase me, I already knew I didn't have the energy to run from them. If such were to happen, with open arms, I would've welcomed my end, but even though coming to terms with this, the strength behind my heart's pound did not lessen.

The stench immediately present walking into the church did not match what it suggested. Movies and TV shows alike always showed that the smell of abandoned death was a horrid unmistakable smell. Thinking this had to be what I was smelling, I looked but saw no bodies along the floor. Not even the ones I thought, as I was being yanked out of the church, were already dead or were sure to approach it soon. Just as it was outside, the result of the fear I remembered seeing was able to still be seen. I didn't have to think about opening a front door. I was able to walk straight through it. After turning on the light when standing at the border of the church's lobby, roaches that looked about the size of my thumb didn't even care to run back into any of the holes that now provided a number of new, irregular decorations along the walls; the roaches seemed to be analyzing me, the newfound intruder of their territory.

It was interesting that after a short time, everything, College Hille, as well as East Knoxville as a whole, to unfamiliar eyes, looked nothing more than the skeleton structure of a portion of a city that once flourished decades ago, but for whatever reason declined or still waited to be cleared out, replaced—possibly, completely gentrified.

She is in there.

As my hands rested on the doors that would lead me into the sanctuary, for a moment, I became stagnant. For days now, whether influenced by fear or not, people, the possible very few that still remained in East, or I guess the entire Knoxville city, had remained unseen and unheard. That said, I wondered. Since that day, I figured had I been the only one to revisit the church, out of respect at least. I knew that I couldn't have been the only one to remember seeing Ms. Darlene's casket, lying like an unwanted item left by the side of a dumpster.

So…what if her casket is still there, several of my thought voices collaboratively questioned.

It was hearing this that struck me harder than anything else I'd heard since running out of the house. I wasn't sure of the answer. Even if I wanted to, burying her by myself was barely an option. Though the church's graveyard provided the space needed, I didn't have a shovel to dig a grave. And then, even if the grave was pre-dug, still the question *so what* rung loudly. I still questioned if I was going to be able to make it back home on the minimal amount of energy I had left. I had just enough to remain standing.

Of the few things, I knew that at the end of funerals, there were usually six or so individuals that carried the casket from the sanctuary. I was barely 120 pounds and was considering the near impossible option of being the only one having to carry a casket that alone looked as though it weighed as much as me. For a brief second, I caught myself inconsiderately wishing Ms. Darlene was cremated. That would've made things a lot easier.

Do you hear yourself? Do you feel yourself, Alex? Ms. Darlene was a provider of the family. What you fear not being able to do does not compare to the difficulties Ms. Darlene reacted to and faced without thought of the obvious difficulty present. Pathetic. Oh yeah, fail.

I wasn't sure if I reacted to these thoughts out of the shame attacking me or if it was out of the irritation of my pride dwindling, but after having come to the decision that even if it took all day and several breaks in between pulls of her casket, I would find a way to bring Ms. Darlene's casket to the graveyard in the back of the church and then, somehow, bury her.

The wider the doors to the sanctuary became as I slowly opened them inch by inch, the wider my eyes became as jolts of shock struck one after another. I looked back and forth from wall to wall for answers.

How?

I sprinted down the aisle. I looked in between the pews to see if an answer could be found despite the small spaces available. Stupidly,

I found that I had briefly looked up towards the ceiling as well. Ms. Darlene's casket still remained there on the floor as nothing more than any of the other broken pieces of trash throughout the sanctuary. It was open. It was open and her body was absent. Still gleaming from the shine I remembered it having, it was just there on the floor looking more like it was still to be bought instead of having already been purchased and used. A combination of confusion and anger began to swarm.

Without thinking, unable to stop myself, I ran out the back of the sanctuary. In an instant, every speck of anger diminished. In an instant, every bit of confusion was unthoughtfully bartered away. Before comprehending the level of stupidity booming from me while bursting through the backdoor of the church, maybe an entire five feet from the door, and now back outside under the blanket of clouds that still remained as a cover stretched from the horizons of opposing sides, I not only again felt the presence of it, I *saw* the embodiment of fear standing there motionlessly.

Run. Run, you idiot. Run!

I couldn't move for what felt like an entire eon. I stood there frozen until the door behind me sharply snapped back against its frame. The body standing there in the close distance shuddered around, but I didn't care to see any more of what had already been seen. Faster than ever before, I sprinted. I discovered the existence of a third wind that could be tapped into with the right amount of drive. My previous exhaustion had never, at all, taken the smallest amount of toll on my body. Right then, I felt that the concept of exhaustion didn't even exist.

"Alex, stop!"

Is this it? Was the first, but wrong, thought.

This is it. Yes. I told myself this was the correct thought.

I ran, no longer aware if I was running to escape from what I knew was closing in behind me or if I was running in hopes of finding the bright light at the end of the tunnel and when found, running even quicker towards it; at this point I demanded to myself that the prolonging of death was the present enemy.

Allow it. It's over.

"Come here!" I heard being yelled as I was swooped from my feet as would be done to a field mouse caught in the grips of a hawk finally breaking its circling of the sky. The hands where calloused and grimy. The embrace the hands had over me felt unbreakable. The embrace feeling unbreakable was uncontested. I didn't care to try to escape. From third wind to no wind, my body reached a level of perfect limpness. I replicated a ragged-doll—nothing less if compared to the ones Ms. Darlene said she took pride in having when she was a toddler.

Cutting behind a house into an alley between East 5th and Woodbine Avenues, I still couldn't find the bright light at the end of the tunnel. I searched thinking that voluntarily blinding myself through looking directly at the sun—ready to ignore any irritation or pain that doing this would bring—would successfully forge a bright light that would at some point morph into this bright light at the end of the tunnel, but this, too, was impossible. The sky, just as it was when I left the house, remained purely overcast. If asked, even the sun couldn't identify my killer.

"Alex, what are you doing out here? Goodness. Look at your foot."

My foot?

Looking down to see my bare feet, blood was gushing effortlessly from my left one. I grew dizzy as I looked up to see that I was in the arms of Mr. Hodge.

"S-Sit down right here."

I heard him clearly but did not, could not move. Everything, emotions, thoughts, absence of Ms. Darlene, Mom, Willie, East Knoxville, everything was slowly being dissected.

"Please," he suggested, but in contradiction to his actions already mandating that I needed to sit down against a wall in the alley.

Still unable to speak, when I looked down again, examining my foot, my new goal was to hold on to any and all of the remaining adrenaline I felt quickly slipping away. It was as if adrenaline was slipping through the same gash that Mr. Hodge had pulled the shard of glass from. I didn't in the least bit remember when it was I stepped on it. For all I knew, it could've been at some point on the way to the church. It could have been during the brief period of running away after seeing who I didn't know was Mr. Hodge. At both periods, I remember being in a state of mind that was close to being absent from reality. At this point though, it didn't matter if I looked towards my blood covered foot or away trying to occupy my mind through searching for a sun that I knew couldn't be directly found. The pain being felt screeched unbearably loud. I could feel it as the tears and sweat on my face became one in the same.

"You think it hurts now, w-wait until you have to put p-peroxide or alcohol on this," Mr. Hodge purposefully chuckled and smiled. In response, I made sure he knew, with the grim, unmoved frown on my face, his attempt failed to lighten the mood.

Nothing more was said while I sat there grappling with bits of rocks, harder and harder as adrenaline left and pain grew. Inhales were becoming as sharp and precise as the shard itself. In refusal to use any of the surroundings to rely on what needed to be done, biting his light green sleeve and pulling his head away and towards the sky as his wrist came down and towards me, eventually the shirt's linen made a scratching sound as it tore from itself.

"This is going to hurt, Alex" he said making sure to look towards me until a brief period of eye contact was made. This was easier said than done. Trying to outdo the pain, I was transferring from eyes being bolted shut to periods where it seemed that my eyelids didn't at all exist. Finally, eye contact between us was made. His miserable look alone tried to prepare me for what was to come.

"Try to lift your leg for just a second, Alex" he rhetorically demanded. Unsure, but more so, not ready for what I knew he was about to do, I watched as he began stretching out the full strand of linen and slowly bringing it closer to my foot that, though not as much as before, was still bleeding considerably. It was all nothing less than a snake approaching and then grasping it victim. His hands approached slowly but swamped my foot with an unforeseen aggression. That pain was so intense, I couldn't find the ability to react to it. The scream I knew was within me was like a burp that was too big and was thus remained entrapped within me.

Watching with the inability to breathe, with the look Mr. Hodge was giving as he glanced regretfully between me and my foot, showing me that he took acknowledgment of my pain; his face told me he made a mistake.

"This is going to hurt, Alex, but this has to be done," he said, but this time avoiding eye contact.

The piece of cloth he tore from his sleeve was not long enough when I looked down and saw him struggling to tie it. After saying this to me, before I could respond, he pulled with a force to basically transform the cloth into a pain like another multi-edged shard of glass piercing me. It felt like the cloth was not only inside of my foot but was just below, almost as if trying to tickle one of my bones. It would have been a blessing to have passed out, but that blessing never came.

"Are you ok?" The pressure never lessened, but finally discontinued to increase. For some time after Mr. Hodge had asked this, I couldn't respond. Unlike ever before, even in comparison to how I felt after initially arriving at College Hille, breath felt like a precious fossil fuel in a quick phase of depletion. It already hurt as I desperately grasped and seemed to at times miss necessary inhales that alone were the differences between life and death. Eyes again bolted and, breathing with a heaviness of two and a half tons, I didn't even try to answer.

Mr. Hodge said nothing more and just sat there across from me in the alley. Bit by bit, the pain was becoming more bearable. I looked down and saw that, though in an extremely small knot sitting at the top of my foot, Mr. Hodge succeeded in covering my wound. Without moving my foot, I could see that the cloth was stained. Blood was no longer pouring or even trickling out. Breaths had finally become slow and deep. I could tell that while it was still strenuous, speaking was now possible.

Breaking the silence, though by the simplest of pieces, stumbling clumsily over words, "What-what are you doing out here, Mr. Hodge?" I was able to throw out in question. Heavy breathing returned.

Answering almost as if he had preplanned the response from already knowing what I would ask him, "No, A-Alex, what are *you* doing out here. Where is your mom? Where is Willie? Are they ok? Why ar—"

"I came to see Ms. Darlene," I interrupted. He waited for me to answer the other questions, but I said nothing else regarding them and instead chose to continue explaining, "I wasn't sure, but I remember how her casket, how she was before we left the funeral. I just wanted to make sure—"

"I had the same thought. She was an amazing woman."

I wanted to ask how he knew her. Of course it may have been as simple as him only knowing of her and her history, so I chose not to say anything and just listened.

"Two days after the funeral, I decided that at the least, s-she deserved to be buried. T-The casket was too heavy so another gentleman and I—with carefulness," he paused overtly emphasizing both his respect for her and his dislike for, what I assumed, how he had to do so, "we picked her body up and gently placed her into where it was that they intended to bury her. Where you saw me standing before you ran off was where we placed her body. I thin—"

It was something about him. I hated it, but I couldn't help it. Every time Mr. Hodge would speak, no matter the topic, I always had a tendency to zone out. Without noticing the blankness I'm sure was blatantly showcased in my eyes, he continued to speak. I continued staring and nodding though barely able to hear a single word.

I noticed though, he was different from the teacher I was used to. Externally, Mr. Hodge was always, even on Casual Fridays of school, the most up-kept man. Whether shining from whichever watch he chose to wear or from light bouncing from the slickness of his shoes—regardless of texture—he was always up-kept. Shirts and pants always looked to have been steam-pressed to the fullest and were *always* topped-off with a bowtie that I noticed he never wore more than twice.

"Mr. Tsunami," me and a few students openly called and ridiculed him the first few weeks of school because of the waves of the 90's he still chose to rock with his short hair. Whether it was genuine or just a way to avoid irritation towards us, when called this, he smiled and answered without any hesitation. Before long though, calling him this died out, but the image of "Mr. Tsunami" continued to be showcased by him.

He often told us that he wanted to be seen as a prototype and further, out of necessity, be part of the reconstructing of the image of those within East Knoxville. There in the ally, as he spoke to me, it was easy to remember him saying this during one of those days in his class, because right there was a man that looked to be desperately holding onto the small amount of strength he still had within him.

Though caught up in the sudden surge of pain after being yanked up by him and even before tearing his sleeve to wrap around my foot, it only took a second to notice the unusualness of Mr. Hodge. Bent over in front of me, that light green button-up shirt was already ripped in places, and noticeably stained. Mr. Tsunami was a thing of the past. His hair was dried with small beads from neglect. He now had what he jokingly critiqued so many students for having. Carelessness.

What is the need to look fancy at such a time? Who is there to be the prototype for and is that really a necessary focus at such a time, Alex? This explanation would've sufficed if the difference I noticed in Mr. Hodge was strictly external. He remained speaking to me and I still remained absent. It seemed that there by my side, absent was also the composure that Mr. Hodge was known for having.

"We come from Kings and Queens," he always reminded us. "Strength is engrained into our DNA. No matter the circumstance, we, especially those of us from East Knoxville, have to remain resilient. I will *always* show my grit. *Always.*" He said this a number of times, word for word, almost as often as the school said the pledge of allegiance. It was easy to see that this was a statement he remembered as many did with their prayers, but like never before, each of the times he previously said this seemed null and hollow. It wasn't extreme, especially in comparison to a student that many called "stutter-bucket," but because it was Mr. Hodge that it was now coming from, it was easy to take notice of. As he continued to speak, he stumbled over even the simplest of words—something he was never known for. Hearing him speak was nerve-wracking. Aside from the stuttering, in between almost every complete sentence was him looking around in anticipation of a presence. When the sound clapped from the door shutting back when we were still at the church, I guess it wasn't absurd for me to wonder if he almost peed himself. It also wasn't absurd to wonder if, when I first took notice of him at the graveyard, was he bent over to be closer to the grave of Ms. Darlene or was he bent over in fear?

"Do you understand, Alex?" he said with a little force to show me he finally took notice of the blankness within my stare. Seeing me snap back to reality, he continued, "There w-were 19 different shootings a-a-around the same time. three of the nineteen happened here in T-Tennessee, and the rest throughout the Eastern coast of the United States. You see what's left here—just in East Knoxville alone. I f-fear that what we see is just from the first sweep of many coming. This emptiness is unrestricted. Fifty-three people have been killed by people said to have been wearing similar c-clothing, b-but the same mask with the same black and white American flag on it and all screaming the same thing as they were apprehended. 'This is Last America.'

"This may be the beginning of America's worst fear. That day, Ms. Darlene's funeral has b-been the only day this has happened— so far. Little information has been given to the public. All we can do is pray and wait, Alex. After years of going to war, I'm afraid the time has come to where it has f-finally come to us."

My heart began dropping far below the streets we were sitting on. After him saying this, all we could do was sit there stuck in a wordless silence present between us, still taking in the wind tickling the leaves attached to the individual branches that birds stood and remained singing on.

"Let's get you home," he smiled. "Do you need me to carry you on my back?"

I guess feeling the need to explain why—based off of the confused look I was purposely giving him—he awkwardly continued, "B-Because of your foot."

Reminded, I took the opportunity and looked down. Consumed by his account of what the news would later call, "the Rebellion," I completely forgot about my foot. Wrapped up, blood looking nothing more than a good grade of paint found on some wall, as much as I wanted to take Mr. Hodge up on this offer, my pride wouldn't allow this. *Stupid.*

"No thank you," I responded smiling. "I think I'll be alright, but would you mind helping me up, sir?"

He only smiled back in response.

With my mouth still closed, I still hissed loudly when I took my first step. That pain was something awful! I was close to collapsing completely. Mr. Hodge gave a concerned look. Just as his mouth began to open, I assume to tell me that his offer still remained on the table, I threw out to him, this time with a forced smile where my teeth were grinding each other, "I think it's time for us to get moving, sir."

His smirk and shaking of his head relayed to me the message that he could easily see through my pride, but that he would comply with my request. "I'd say you're right, Alex. L-Let's get moving."

"This is where I live," was the only simple sentence said between us as we walked down the streets on the way back home. It was feeble. I didn't know Mr. Hodge lived this close to where we lived, but at the same time, I never, and still at that moment, couldn't find the sense to care. I said nothing back and only nodded out of respect. Nothing more was said as we... as he walked and I limped.

I must've been running at a crazy speed because, not even taking into consideration that my foot obviously slowed us down considerably, it still took an extreme amount of time to even come within view of my house. The journey back remained nerve wracking. The silence and absence of people along the streets added to the chill that was already present in response to the overcast. Clouds remained stretched out perfectly. Individual clouds, if even multiple ones were present, could not be distinguished from one another. Grey instead of the consistent tint of blue that could be seen on a cloudless day—this was what the overcast copied.

What was even worse than the absence of people was the fear of what the sudden presence of a person could mean. Still jerky as he was when I first noticed, at random moments, Mr. Hodge's head would pull away from in front of us with such suddenness that I thought I might've possibly heard his neck snap. Every one of the different times he did this, I got goosebumps all the same, and was instantly ready to endure the pain I knew would come from running. A few of the times he snapped his head away towards an area it was only the sound from a stray animal that he turned towards, and also turned whatever animal it was we saw—whether a dog, cat, or squirrel—towards us. More times than not, when Mr. Hodge snapped his neck, not only did I not hear anything to begin with, but when following the direction he was looking, I saw nothing and concluded there was nothing to see to begin with. I didn't fault him for this, but I wondered if I would soon become overwhelmed and submissive to the same paranoia.

Finally we were back at the corner of Jefferson Avenue and Milligan Street. My house could be seen. I limped a few steps before I realized that Mr. Hodge was no longer next to me.

"I think it's fine to assume that you can make it back to your house safely from here on." As he began slightly straightening up his posture, lowering his shoulders as he lifted his chin towards the rooftops of close-by houses, he said to me, "Tell your mother. . .and Willie," he seemed to have forgotten, but quickly remembered to say, "that I said hello and that if she, you all need me, you know where I stay." As he finished these last words, without waiting for any response of acknowledgement from me, he was already turned around walking back towards East 5th.

The door was shut but unlocked. The sky was nowhere near as dim as I remembered it being when I first left the house. Whereas the sun had also been concealed by thicker clouds than when I returned, it was now towards the middle-point of the sky. Before walking in, the sun looked like a shiny marble. Clouds made it easy to look directly at it without any straining or irritation.

"Mom, Willie, I'm back," I whispered as I crept through the door in hopes of doing away with any of the possible fear that it wasn't me that they heard walking through the front door. Before the door was completely opened, Willie almost tackled me.

Interrupted by uncontrollable tears I could feel that were dampening my shoulders, "W-we t-t-t-thought they t-took you! Where d-d-did you go?" He sounded so similar to how Mr. Hodge sounded, but sounded so for a different reason. Fully dressed, Mom slowly cut around the corner of the living room. She said nothing, but only stood there. From across the room, I could see dried streaks on her cheeks. Not breaking eye contact toward me, not even from a single blink or twitch from either of her eyes, I could see gratefulness quickly overcoming the fear that was once present, but then just as quickly as the gratefulness overcame fear, standing still and saying nothing, minimally shaking her head, that gratefulness was being substituted with rage. Her face called me every synonym for "stupid, idiotic, selfish child of mine." Still having not said a word, she simply turned to head back towards the stairs.

"What happened to your foot," Willie questionably exclaimed. "It's been bleeding!"

Before fully walking out from vision, Mom turned and looked down towards my wrapping. Taking notice of the blood-stained cloth there, following a deep inhale from surprise, even more rage engulfed her and her eyes cut even deeper into me.

"I ran over-I felt that-Mr. Hodge-When I saw-College Hille-The dented tricycle-" Not knowing what to say first, I stumbled, in absolutely no chronological order of my recent journey. Thought became more meshed together as Mom approached closer. Reaching, still having not said a word nor breaking her stare towards me and before placing her hand, I was looking around the room frantically. At this point, I was more afraid of Mom than I ever was, at any point, outside.

She sympathetically took hold of me, and led me over to the couch. Her grip ripped out every word I could think to say.

"Lift up your leg. Let me see your foot, Alex," she said no longer looking at me.

Of course complying, I did as she asked. When she nipped with her sharp nails and untied the cloth to examine my foot, her eyes widened for a second I guess in shock of what she was now looking at.

"I'm sorry, Mom!" I finally found the courage to blurt out.

She paused for second and became motionless with my foot in her hand. "I know," was all she calmly said to me. Nothing more was said between us for the remainder of day. In a sense, I was okay with that.

"Go get the alcohol, Willie," she mandated.

14

Few words remained to be said between me and Mom. I gave her her space long after I returned. The pain I caused her was obvious, but regardless, I didn't regret doing what I did in the least bit. On the contrary, I was sort of proud of myself. Out of love and respect, I ran to the far end of East Knoxville, despite a danger I wasn't sure was absent or present. I ran ready to provide what I knew a loved one deserved. It was unfortunate that one of the effects from doing this also fractured the bridge connecting me and Mom.

At the same time, the bridge was only fractured and fortunately not demolished. If it had been demolished, nothing would be said between us—at all. Though, for days, it felt like nothing more than an emotionless "Are you hungry, Willie, Alex," I felt a sensation of relief that my name, my inclusion, was a significant portion within these five words.

The bridge between me and Willie was unchanged. If there was any change to the bridge between us two, it was unnoticeable—

nothing more than a bridge after someone throws a rock from the bridge over into the river.

Days since Ms. Darlene's funeral turned into weeks. Whereas at one point, silence remained undisrupted, the humming of cars, though small and barely noticeable at first, began to return. Every so often, sirens were also heard. I took this as a signal that the emergency vehicles the sirens belonged to were first going to a tragedy involving people, and second, within distance. We were no longer *completely* alone in Knoxville.

Things began changing back drastically. The humming of cars in the distance no longer remained far away, only on the interstate. Used to the loud silence I had grown accustomed to, though two avenues from Magnolia, it seemed like I grew the ability to tell the precise location of cars gradually beginning to zoom up and down.

In front of Pilot.

Interesting, they, pertaining to whoever it was in the car, *have stopped at the stoplight on the block of Milligan and Magnolia.*

It was one day we were all sitting in the living room. Willie was on his I-Pad playing one of his random games. The seemingly obvious understanding that was unquestionably abided by the vast majority of Knoxville was the rule: *Don't leave home.* It was like everyone, grown-ups as well, were back in public school and were experiencing an unforeseen snow blizzard; in Knoxville a "snow blizzard" was only two or so inches. Due to a feared danger that no one had seen anymore of, still, to leave home was presumed to be risking life. That being said, with now having all of the time in the world, Mom was on the couch reading a book she long desired to read—*The Alchemist.* I was simply stretched out on the floor saying nothing.

Mom no longer strictly enforced the silent rule. I never worried about it, but Willie, on the other hand, for whatever reason, found reasons to get excited, and whenever he did, his voice would always be there, on the border of yelling.

"Willie," was all Mom had to say whenever he would reach this point of excitement. This time though she said nothing.

"Ahhhh!…Dannng!…..I was so close!…..R-Right there." Willie was saying to himself with eyes all but glued to the screen of his I-Pad.

"You know what I hate about this game, Alex?" Willie began, as if I knew a single thing about the game he was playing.

"What's that?"

"Every time I play this level, every single time, I get closer and closer, but I can't seem to get past this level. I wish this stup—"

"What was that," Mom shot up from the couch. "Shut up! Did you hear that, Alex?"

I had no idea what she was talking about, but the shock in her eyes, caused the return of an almost forgotten fear.

"Stay here. Watch Willie," She said hastily tip-toeing to the kitchen.

Unable to stay there, curious to what had caused this reaction from her, I commanded that Willie stayed there in the living room and followed close behind Mom.

"What in the world is this" I heard her whisper to herself as she stood jittering and looking out of the kitchen window.

"What is it Mom?"

She turned so sharply, I still don't understand how the momentum from her head's turn didn't twist her body in a full circle. With eyes widened to the point of explosion being on the horizon, they only grew wider when she then looked passed me. There was Willie looking pathetically scared with his arms wrapped around himself. The only one that could get mad was Mom. I couldn't get mad at Willie. He followed me just as I followed her.

"Wha—" she began, but didn't finish igniting whatever explosion me and Willie were soon to surely die from. Just as she started, her attention went back to whatever it was on the other side of the kitchen window.

Curiosity controlled both me and Willie. Despite the fear of possibly being smacked back to my senses and back to the church, and to the tomb joining Ms. Darlene, we were there next to Mom looking for what she was focused so intensely on.

"Is that them," Willie pulled on my sleeve asking.

Shock pounded one time against my heart when I finally saw what she saw and began hearing what she heard. Right there, going up and down the street in a careless, but searching manner, was little Miguel and his younger sister Rachel, the son and daughter of our neighbors two houses down. She was on her bicycle, he was chasing her hopping up and down the street with a growing laugh containing a sound that could be heard within a decent distance.

"Are they crazy?"

"I think they are," Willie voluntarily answered, though I wasn't speaking to him.

I waited for Mom to say something, but she continued to look out of the window with a completely baffled look engraved on her face.

Part of me seeing them and furthermore seeing them outside, brought an incomparable feeling of hope. Their father, who I finally was able to locate sitting on the bottom step of their house, was a soldier. The most I knew of the Rebels was nothing more than what Mr. Hodge briefly told me on the walk back from the church. Out of fear, our TV remained off, even if that meant keeping us from possibly knowing more about the recent events.

This all being said, using what I felt was plausible logic, surely if anyone had a critical understanding regarding all that was then going on, it would be Mr. Sanchez, who was outside, with his children allowing them to scream at the top of their lungs.

Are we safe? Is it all over?

I was sincerely hoping that is was. We hadn't cooked anything since the funeral. Breakfast, lunch, dinner, if all three were even had during the same day, consisted of cereal, canned foods, and bags of off-branded chips that were already stale prior to all this. I never openly asked Mom, but every day, I wondered how we would've gone about getting food once we had no more—which would've been soon. I could tell Mom also contemplated this. Her servings of food grew smaller by the day.

"Mommy, can I go outside, too?"

I waited for Mom's response just as eagerly as Willie did. While Mr. Sanchez sat there without a smile on his face, but this was how he usually looked. Though he had no smile, there seemed to be no sense of fear or worry in him either. There were no jitters or constant looking around as was done by Mr. Hodge.

"No."

"But they are outsi—"

Interrupting with the precision of knife, "Willie," was all she said before finally walking off upstairs. "Get away from and don't go back to the window," she directed before we began to hear the creaks from each step as she walked to her room.

All it took was an event two days later for things to change dramatically and almost instantly in Knoxville and I'm sure in America as a whole.

Though each of the many times Willie asked to go outside were easily declined, Mom at least eventually approved of the TV being turned on just as long as it couldn't be heard in other rooms. It wasn't until the nights, when Willie would finally pass out that Mom felt comfortable turning to the news station in hopes of learning a little more about the Rebels.

The same "This is last America," screeched by the same Rebel was all that was replayed on each of the different news stations. On this video replayed for the 100th time, the date showed in it remained the same. After weeks later, it remained that nothing more was learned—that or nothing more was shared.

"This is last—"

"We have breaking news," a news reporter broke in one night. It was just after 10 o'clock. Willie was asleep on the couch. Both me and Mom were startled. The news reporter looked as though he had heard and was ready to share to audiences everywhere the worst news able to be provided since the first attack. I prepared myself

"It saddens me to reveal to you, my fellow Americans…" As he spoke, it felt almost as though I was there, sharing the same studio the reporter sat in. He paused looking back down to the papers held in his hands as if confirming the tragedy he was getting ready to reveal to us. We waited for what seemed like hours.

Bombs? More Rebels? Mass shootings? What?

The anchor finally looking back at the camera, looking almost square in the eyes of every person watching, "Confirmed at 9:17pm, America has lost renowned, Hall of Fame athlete…"

I had never heard of whoever it was that he stated had died. Maybe if Ms. Darlene was still alive, she would be able to educate me on who it was. I asked Mom who this athlete was. With eyebrows scrunched almost into a uni-brow and eyes able to be seen switching from side to side, she said nothing.

Changing between different news stations, there was nothing more of the Rebels, their individual attacks, or the deaths brought forth by any of the separate ones were further mentioned. Officially, all of the past few weeks was a thing of the past. The focus of our America had finally shifted to something that the news suggested was of equal importance—the death of one athlete, that was finally stated to have come in the form of a stroke.

Mom said nothing more, but instead turned the TV off and sat back against the wall with her eyes closed. The only way I knew she hadn't fallen asleep was because of the excessive bouncing of her knee as she sat there one leg crossed over the other.

Time went on and days continued to pass day after day until becoming week after week since the city alarm disrupted Ms.

Darlene's funeral, and furthermore since what seemed to have more importance, the death of the somewhat renowned athlete I never cared to remember. With this passing of time, it was almost as if the alarm was nothing more than a nightmare that never happened. It was a topic and event that was silently confirmed, never again to be brought up between me, Mom and Willie as well as the rest of Knoxville, as if at some point we had all signed some kind of a blood contract preventing further mentioning of it.

It was now mid-August. Though no longer having the three jobs she previously found some way to balance, Mom still went back to having two jobs. It didn't take much to see that Knoxville as a whole suffered tremendous amounts of damage. Ironically, the vast majority of damage that could be seen was deemed to have come from those of Knoxville. The wrecks, the fires, houses and buildings broken into were scattered throughout the city.

"Are you ready to go help, Alex?" Willie asked one morning.

"Let's go," I managed to answer, though deep down, I wished I felt comfortable enough to allow him to go out on his own.

It was interesting that based off of what could still be seen, you'd imagine that our Concrete Jungle, East Knoxville, was the portion of Knoxville most viciously damaged. As time continued to pass and small amounts of reconstruction, provided by government funding, began to happen, the damage present in East Knoxville, in comparison to other portions of Knoxville seemed to take the longest to clean up.

Teachers, officers, parents, pastors and even some of the homeless sometimes seen walking up and down the streets talking to themselves about it, all took notice that it seemed that we remained close to untouched by any of the city's assistance. It was ironic that this was true. This provided an opportunity to see what was often overlooked pertaining to the Concrete Jungle, East Knoxville.

Sometimes, because of the perception of us, even we forgot the beauty that was deep in this portion of the city. Fortunately, at this critical time, we, East Knoxville, remembered the grit we had as a community; what we felt was incomparable to any amounts of money that was continuing to be provided to the other communities. After some took notice of this unequal attention, what started with a few, was soon a responsibility voluntarily adopted by many.

Internal food drives and neighborhood clean-ups continuously began taking our community by storm.

Several times I saw people tired, angry, saddened, but none of these feelings could long outdo the comprehension that people, regardless of financial status, were capable of a selflessness that could and often did provide the difference in the life of someone else. Because of this, any emotion or feeling that potentially blocked the productivity of the work still seen to be done throughout the neighborhoods of East Knoxville was only temporary in what soon became the vast majority of the community.

One of the first things I remember was a cookout done at the top of Chilhowee Park. There was no way that the church that planned this expected the number of people that came. Mom was at work, but still told me and Willie that we should go. Considering the time she would've gotten off work, I thought me and Willie would've been able to attend, eat, socialize and get back regardless of if she told us we could or couldn't go. We would've went regardless, but it was good she permitted this because when we got back home, she was already there.

By the time we got to the cook-out in the early evening, it already looked like two separate schools' field days were being hosted in one area. They had run out of food three times before we got any. While there was food, music, and games present, the main goal of this event we finally found out was to encourage and ask for help in cleaning up our home—East Knoxville. In the audience, though predominantly black, space was shared by the tall and short, the scruffy and tidied, the hairy and bald, young and old, the dark-skinned and the light-skinned, the hetero and the homosexual; at Chilhowee, were believers in God, Allah, Aja, Rah, no God, and all gods. The inclusivity present during this cook-out was seen and acknowledged, but not focused on. During this time, unlike ever before where we needed to collaborate together, we collectively established that our presence signified unconditional responsibility. *All* of it.

Eventually, the music was silenced, the games were forced to pause. Given a microphone to speak to us, the audience, we, too, quickly became silent. A woman walked up towards a small podium and began speaking.

"They said she lost her daughter," I overheard someone next to me fail to whisper to someone.

From hearing this, I wondered could this have been the mother of the child that the broken tricycle belonged to? Considering, even if small, the slight possibility of this, I stood there ready for whatever it was she was soon to tell us.

"If we don't first care about our streets," she began, close to yelling with tears already flushing her eyes under the slightly-clouded, full moon-lit night above us, "what does it matter if no one else does? It seems to be obvious that our home, East Knoxville, is not even the slightest priority for the city's reconstruction plan."

She wasn't any pastor that I knew of, but still received the responses known to be given to the pastor of the most energetic church. Yells from many remained being felt as she continued to speak and challenge us.

Finally asking for a full commitment from everyone to contribute in some shape, form, or fashion, to our own reconstruction, Willie interrupted, "Can we help, too, Alex?"

Smiling to him, all I gave was a nod.

This night contained the beauty and unmatchable strength many deprived the supposed Concrete Jungle of. This night was the beginning of showing a beauty that many of those of East Knoxville failed to remember had at one time been present within our streets. Finally walking all the way home, despite the slight but consistent sting still present in my foot, holding hands with Willie, with a newfound drive and resurfaced reason to contribute, and regardless of the perceptions had of our home, we walked down the streets with pride. I *am*, we *are* from East Knoxville, the Concrete Jungle, the Land of Nightmares, and as I always felt, further confirming to myself, I wouldn't have it any other way.

For the following days and weeks—the remainder of the summer—the constant helping would at times grow tiresome and I often needed to remind myself that I wasn't working solely for my betterment.

We got home still embraced by a beauty I wish could've lasted longer than a few more weeks. Though covered by many suns, it was soon that I would again take special notice of the sun's gorgeous smile.

15

THE RETURN:
AUGUST 31

Things grew back to normal. School had started back. Consistent, week after week of community volunteering in East Knoxville still didn't compare to the reconstruction other parts of the city were being blessed with. It wasn't the actual hard work that was wearing people out. Sometimes, through the eyes of many, as well as mine and Willie's, even after hours during some weekday evenings and weekend afternoons, under a scorching quilt of heat, progress never seemed to be made.

Eventually, even city and county clean-up forces joined our efforts. Cars and trucks still abandoned on the sides of streets and the others that were still cluttering parking lots of businesses were slowly but eventually cleared car by car. Though finally receiving a once neglected help, there was only so much able to be done for many. Cleaning up trash from street corners and abandoned cars being cleared away didn't and couldn't replace the cars that some still needed. Hours of cleaning up couldn't replace the knocked out windows that some houses were stuck with—especially during the rains that were sure to continue coming through.

Though we weren't ridiculed by many, some still took the opportunity to throw jokes at me, or more so isolate me from them and others during lunch and in between class changes.

"You don't know *our* struggle," was the foundation of the ridicule that was just altered slightly as it came from the mouths of a few.

The weird thing I had to accept was that these simple-minded attacks were true. I didn't know. No matter how long or how many days I cleaned, no matter how appreciative people continuously made me feel, or even how great it was to see Willie smile when he took notice of me overcoming my obvious desire to stay in bed sleeping—especially on those weekend afternoons—none of that mattered. I didn't know how they felt.

Again, though I lived in the same East Knoxville that many who ridiculed me lived in, there were two parts of East Knoxville. Depending on which part someone lived in, this was something that could leave a noticeable impact on people's perception. I was never sure where the exact point began, but sometimes, just to make judgement slightly easier, a section cut off by Cherry Street and Magnolia was the unofficial boundary between what many deemed "us vs them." The city didn't make escaping this judgement any easier. In fact, it almost made escaping this judgement impossible.

Though thankful for all that we had, and all that Ms. Darlene did and provided us with, sometimes people made it seem as though it was okay to question if all we had was a blessing or if it all was actually a curse. Before everything happened, it could've already been easily argued that one side of East Knoxville was not and should not be considered part of the Concrete Jungle. After everything happened, that same question existed and even I was one of the ones asking.

Starting on Cherry Street and walking a few streets over, visually things changed drastically. The suburbs began. As a whole, we continued to clean, but around where we lived was barely touched by us because we didn't need it. Somehow escaping much of the damage other portions of the city as a whole suffered, even the bits surrounding houses that did endure, in our section of East Knoxville, it was quickly cleaned, and as it was, I noticed this just as other classmates did.

Two days back into school from summer break and I was already suspended.

"You aren't black."

Something like this would've always made me furious, but at a time like this, my temper exploded.

Clearly enraged but trying her hardest and failing to give off only an upset vibe, Mom said on the ride home from picking me up from school, "That's oka—no it's not okay, but I'm going to make this okay, Alex. You about to work your tail off for these next three days. I guarantee you this!"

Due to my discipline record from previous years, and possibly in collaboration with my record from when I was in middle school, Mom told me I was blessed and that I should've been gone for far longer. Though never told for how long and never cared to find out, I believed this without a doubt.

"You better thank Mr. Hodge next time you see him, Alex. He told me he defended you and was able to get you out of the trouble you deserved. You are smart. You're smarter than the average teenager your age, but sometimes you do and allow the dumbest things to influence and provoke you into doing things that are just as dumb. To thank Mr. Hodge, aside from the lawns that you have started to cut, you are going to cut his—for free."

I didn't mind this, but it was only one time and a half that I'd be able to cut Mr. Hodge's yard.

During the second time I was cutting Mr. Hodge's yard, as I started, I kept wishing that I had mowed his yard earlier in the week. Considering how smart I was, this day was make it or break it. I couldn't hold off from cutting his yard any longer. Well, I could've, but considering the older lawn mower I remembered seeing he had from the first time I cut his grass, I knew that waiting any longer would've been, as Mom would deem, "a dumb decision made by a smart person." Usually, though a decent distance, I wouldn't have minded rolling our personal lawn mower to his yard as I had done the first time cutting his and as I had done with other yards—some about the same and others even farther distances. On this day, the temperature was 97 degrees and felt like it was at least 10 degrees past 100. The sun itself was laughing and after every chuckle, a pulse of heat was pushed against me. I refused to roll our lawnmower all the way to his house under this heat. I chose to walk there and just use his. Initially, though able to see that his was old, I figured it was still usable. Mistake.

On this day, I had finally made it to Mr. Hodge's yard. For no reason other than having to cut the grass in this heat—though it was my fault—I wasn't in the best of moods. Though I saw that his car was in his backyard, I chose not to knock on his door to tell him I was here; I chose not to even bother simply asking him how he was doing. Completely out of nowhere, I was extremely irritable. I was sweaty, tired, and thirsty. For no reason at all, he was my designated scapegoat.

To top off the irritation I was already feeling, when I got his old, burst down, rust-on-almost-every-square-inch lawn mower, I couldn't get it started. I checked the gas, but it was full. I looked under it not completely knowing what it was I was looking for, hoping to become the mechanic I knew full well I wasn't.

After hearing the front door open and the hearing woodened porch accented footsteps of Mr. Hodge coming to the edge just before the steps, he just stood there watching me struggle.

Primarily I thought, *Now you see me struggling with this broke down thing of yours*, but then I half way got mad when he finally asked, "You need help, Alex?"

Pride always was my weakness.

"I got it, Mr. Hodge," I snapped back as I continued yanking the chord harder than the previous pull.

I'm strong enough, sir.

Before I knew it, it felt like I had already cut five or so yards before I even began to mow.

More than likely, out of response from seeing the amount of sweat slipping from every one of my pores, he began to ask "Would you like me to get you a glass of water, Al—"

Before he could finish and before I could insinuate that I still didn't need his help, not sure what it was I did differently, the motor finally coughed into a steady groan. Having to make sure I didn't even look at him through my peripheral, I acted as though the starting of the lawnmower distracted and prevented me from fully hearing his generosity. But in all honesty, considering how hard it was to get that thing started, even if I wasn't in a bad mood, unless he was going to stand next to me with a glass of water in hand and hold a straw up to my mouth, I refused to let go and allow his contraption to shut off again. Refusing to acknowledge that I heard him—despite how great a glass of water would've been—was the efficient route that seemed to make things a lot easier considering how I was feeling.

As my scapegoat for how I was feeling from both the annoyance at having to be there and feeling like I was being cooked in a stir-fry, all I could manage to think about was my rough first impression with Mr. Hodge. At that time, I had been a freshman and he was still a sophomore English teacher. It was the first day at school, and even more important to me, it was my first day in high school.

Sirens

Unlike ever before, simply based off of stories heard about the school, I felt I had to establish, regardless of how, an image that I was of the stronger if not the strongest freshman. Looking for absolutely any way to begin molding the perception I wanted the school to have of me, stupidly, purposefully, I ran into a junior athlete whose nickname was "Psycho." In middle school, I was petrified whenever I heard the stories of him and the pain he was said to have left people feeling after tackling them during games—and even sometimes during practices.

Seeing the opportunity ahead during that first day of school, he was walking down the middle of the hallway after the first bell rang and everyone was heading to their first class. Because he was so popular, though he and the other athletes took up over half the hallway, students did not hesitate to get out their way, but not me. Us two, we had to have looked like a midget and a giant walking towards each other. As we continued walking towards one another, he took no notice of me until finally, BAM! He about knocked me off my feet, and although he knocked my books everywhere, I remained standing. We both stopped walking.

I was ready to retaliate regardless of what I imagined he was sure to say or do in response.

Sirens.

"Dang, dude!" I overtly strived to yell in hopes that the entire hallway heard and shifted focus. Several eyes suddenly cut over to see and take in what had happened before anything else happened.

In complete contrast to what I thought he would do, with a huge smile he was already apologizing and bending down to pick up the books that he mistakenly thought he knocked down. In reality, I kind of threw them down—to add emphasis.

Before being able to get back up from voluntarily picking up my textbooks, I shoved him back down, along with my books, to the tiles. Before, eyes were on us, but after this, eyes were *stuck* on us as bodies began to surround us.

Silence that swarmed the hallways was broken only by me exclaiming, "Don't be bumping into me, dude. I ain't one of these other people scared of you!"

He remained down on the tiles in an absolute confusion. Completely contrary to how I thought he would respond, he snickered with a smirk suggesting he didn't have time for this. As he started to get back up, I took a step towards him to push him back down, but with hands in front of me, ready for contact, between two jerks of a single eyeball, school security guard, Officer Troy, had both of my hands in his grasp and was already escorting me down to the main office to wait for the principal.

Sirens.

Groan.

Sirens.

As I sat there for what seemed like forever, nonchalantly came Mr. Hodge walking through the office door.

Before noticing me, Mr. Hodge said, "Good morning, sir. Is boss man back there?"

Saying nothing, all Officer Troy did was shortly shake his head to both sides only once.

Then turning and seeing me, Mr. Hodge jokingly said to Officer Troy, "School has barely started and you already got one? That says a lot about this school year, sir."

With only a chuckle, which I thought was forged, "Who you telling, Hodge," was all Officer Troy said back to him.

"Wait, I know you," Mr. Hodge then said to me. I never cared to ask him how it was that he knew me before I knew him. Welcomingly, he continued, "My name is Mr. Hodge."

"Did I ask," I whispered.

At that point, every bit of politeness drained out of him.

"Yes, I know you very well, Alexand—"

"It's *Alex*," I said still not caring to look at him with any respect.

"Look, I'm not your enemy," he began. "I'm sorry you've found yourself in trouble already, but one thing is for certain, I won't be disrespected, Alexand—"

"It's *Alex!*" I instinctively shouted. I was then looking him square in the eyes.

Disbelief widened his now intimidating eyes. People saying my full name has always been *the* pet peeve; people think they know so much about someone from simply knowing their name. I knew that how I said this came off as disrespectful. I felt an urge to apologize because he didn't know this, but something prevented me from doing this that day. From that point on, until the following year that I found myself in his class, words never left from one to the other in conversation. Our body languages were more than enough. Standing there in the office, the arching of the left side of his mouth, the tightening of my eyes, the lifting of his chest, as if he were some kind of a contemporary Hercules, these were all the words that needed to be said that day.

This first impression was two years ago. Though during that year we never personally spoke, when I found myself in his class we were both prepared for what we both knew would be a rough year between us, but I think to both of our surprise, it was the complete opposite.

"You are a phenomenal student, Alexand—*Alex!*" He emphasized his consideration of my name request.

It wasn't until later that I learned that Mr. Hodge saying this was the worst blessing. He did all but officially tell me that I was his favorite student, and with becoming this came higher expectations. In an overt way, he was always stricter towards me. Sometimes, other classmates didn't work half as hard as I would on an assignment, but would still make better grades. There were times when an "A" grade for them was a "B-" or maybe even a "C" grade for me. It was annoying.

"It's not fair," I remember once complaining to Mom. I told her this in hopes that she would march down, guns blazing, demanding answers as to why I was not being treated same as the rest of the students.

Just as it was when I tried to provoke the athlete on the first day of school, in absolute complete contrast to what I felt would be done by Mom after I had told her of Mr. Hodge, aside from the gentle smile shown, all she said was, "You'll thank him one day."

To this very moment, I'm not sure if I missed something, but even after considering that possibility, that day never came.

Sirens

Sirens

Groan—cough—groan

Sirens

"Take this," I remember Mr. Hodge saying to me after I finished cutting his grass the first time, "but don't tell your mother." In his extended hand was a twenty dollar bill.

After giving me the money, he explained to me that despite the punishment he knew I was in with having to cut his grass, he told my mom that he didn't mind paying me to cut his yard.

"She wouldn't budge, Alex, but still," he said with his arm extended, "you deserve it—just don't tell you mother. I fear her as much as you should," he said while laughing.

"Thank you," was all I said before pushing our lawnmower back home that evening.

When it was time to cut his grass this second time, though irritated and already tired before I even started, I came sure that he would offer the same amount, but even if he offered more money, for whatever reason, I was sure I wouldn't have taken it. As the evening continued, and within the short amount of time I was there cutting, the agitation I was feeling did nothing but increase drastically until I wasn't sure whether or not I was actually mad. I was in no mood to show even the slightest sense of happiness—stupidity, stubbornness. Again, Mr. Hodge was my scapegoat. As soon as the lawnmower finally started and I found myself fully drifted into deep thought remembering our first impression, I had fully intended to keep Mr. Hodge as the scapegoat.

Then it all started.

That evening, I cut his grass while my skin was surely being darkened and the sun continued chuckling. Only about ten minutes in, I snapped out of daydreaming when three police cars zoomed down the street with their sirens singing loudly. Looking up, the sun seemed to finally begin its transition to its setting phase. As the lawnmower's motor continued to groan, a few streets over, though still hearing the sirens of the three police cars that recently passed, I heard a number of other sirens, distinguishable from one another, passing one another. I could tell that while some were heading in the same direction as the police cars I had just seen, others were also coming from that direction. Then it was heard. From all directions, the emergency sirens began to contribute to, similar to how the synchronization was when I was running to the church to see Ms. Darlene one last time—one constant, steady, untiring scream.

By then, drops of sweat were plunging from every jumpable edge of my body. Swarmed with anxiety, hands were gripped on the handle so tight that they were at the point where my arms started to join my legs' trembling. As the emergency sirens heightened their scream, out of nowhere came a thunder vibrating even the ground I was standing on. Not a *single* cloud was anywhere in sight, but undeniably, an unforgettable thunderous pound pushed against my body. Following this came a resonating crack that finally broke my hands from the lawnmower. Though having no clue where it came from or was heading, I left the lawnmower and began my sprint home.

It felt as though, right then, I wasn't just feeling it, but instead I became, I was adrenaline.

"Alex!" I heard Mr. Hodge yell.

By the time he came out to the porch and called for me, I was already three or so houses down the street. I think completely unrelated to how broken down and old it was, but instead out of response to the speed I found myself running at, I was almost five houses down the street before I took notice of lawnmower's groan finally dying out.

People, families were running and jumping behind the steering wheels that allowed their horns to join the ones now yelling in bulk. Running, reaching, then leaving the blocks of the neighborhood, it seemed that after people had hopped in their cars their acceleration sometimes happened so quickly, I didn't notice first hearing their engines' beginning cranks.

At the top of my lungs, I screamed, "Willie!"

Finally, cutting the corner, from Milligan and streaming up Jefferson Ave., our lawn in full view, I saw him laid out. Right there, Willie was flat out on the ground of our yard. At that moment, what I only before saw and easily neglected on the news, what I was finally able to force in becoming as distant and irrelevant as a nightmare, suddenly became a reality standing in front of me.

Seeming to be a part of what the news called the "Rebels," this individual stood there wearing all white. Instant paralysis as the person standing in *my* yard turned their head towards me. I didn't move. I was barely breathing. I was making eye contact with uncovered eyes behind the mask that had that crippling, subtle expression able to scare me even from behind the TV screen. This person was looking towards me, but still had a gun pointed at Willie.

Time all but froze. Every passing millisecond felt like several hours. I remembered, long ago, accepting the responsibility of protecting Willie. I claimed I would be there to provide—no matter what, even at the cost of my life. I deemed that my purpose in life would forevermore be to ensure his safety. Milliseconds passed by, and these thoughts continued to remind me that I was a failure. I couldn't move as I felt the biting sensation of having to accept what was becoming.

Failure, Alex. Complete. Full. Perfect failure.

After things began to settle down in Knoxville, based off of what she supposedly learned from talks with Mr. Sanchez, several times Mom tried to inform me with all that she finally knew. Mom tried to inform me about the separate killings that all happened on that same day as the funeral , but with forcing the thought that it was nothing more than an event that would never again happen, out of repression, I never did and always refused to pay attention.

Still stuck, as if he were right there knelt down on one knee with one arm on my shoulder seeing the same thing I was, I heard Mr. Hodge's famous line "People don't care until it's at their front door." At this moment, remembering this made me dizzy. I wanted to throw up. It was too coincidental that all that I was seeing, right then, was literally happening *at my front door* and unlike any time before, *I cared*. It was too late. Though it wouldn't have mattered much at this moment, I remember wishing I knew more of the person that these eyes I was making direct contact with belonged to, but I didn't.

Every bit of the helplessness I felt was in direct response to the self-induced hypnosis I'd mastered. After all that had happened, I felt that I, we—Willie, myself, and Mom—were all unofficially safe; I felt there was some unbreakable wall established and thus preventing any and all future danger from coming. And yet there I stood.

Stupid, I heard several of my thoughts in many different voices screaming to me. What felt like hours of stagnation, unable to even twitch a finger, was not a single passing of a second. It was as if both feet were seemingly attached to the street I stood on, while at the same time, as though I was there watching side by side with the sun, I was hearing its laughter as we watched something too far away to make even the slightest difference.

Breaking the grip that encompassed me, "Willie!" was screamed as the front door flung open. Because the door flung open so quickly and with so much force, at almost the same time, another crack was sent resonating towards the unreachable horizon. I opened my eyes not yet realizing how tightly I had closed them. Breaking bolts as my eyes grew wider, I was scared to look up and confirm whether the crack heard was the screen door hitting the wall. Deep down I knew where the crack came from.

Within the time it took for a single exhale, three bodies were now there laid out on the ground. Nausea continued to overwhelm me until I was on the ground finally emptily throwing up food I hadn't even eaten; everything swirled in constant motion as a number of emergency sirens continued singing, accompanying other spontaneous cracks streets down. I struggled with not being able tell whether the ones I was hearing were travelling echoes or separate cracks just distanced from the one heard and the ones shortly following.

Able to somewhat balance myself again, I stammered towards each of the motionless bodies there in the yard. Though ready to release every tear beating against my eyelids, the emotion quickly dissipated. When I crawled towards Willie there was no blood. Just a constant soft breathing and this placement of Willie's body was familiar. I wanted to punch him. As extreme as the fury was that blasted through me right then, it was extinguished by the realization that, most likely in response to fear, that boy, my brother, had simply passed out. Bent over him, I also smelled the strong stench left from him peeing on himself.

The Rebel was different, though. Finally close enough to see that the Rebel was a woman, in our yard, *she* was nothing more than a misplaced boulder. If this Rebel was a boulder, the butcher knife Mom found enough energy to bury so deeply, firmly in her was nothing less than the sword it would take a King Arthur to pull out.

Out of nowhere, I felt a strange desire. While the brown, silky thin hair of the Rebel continued to be lifted and transferred from side to side by wind being blown over us, this was all that moved on the Rebel's body. I *knew* the Rebel was dead. With this confirmation,

I wanted to see *who* this Rebel was in particular. Behind the mask I knew was a lady. Behind this mask was a lady that, to my understanding, chose to become a part of the fear that was taking the surrounding streets by storm. I wanted to confirm that behind this mask was a face that was even uglier than the things being done; a face that would disgust me more than what was felt after Ms. Darlene's funeral was interrupted. I wanted this but it wasn't the case. In that brief moment of eye contact I made with this warm hazel-eyed lady, I felt the possibility that she may have been nothing less than your everyday smiling pretty girl walking in a grocery store somewhere.

Succumbing to the excruciating desire to see what it was that could be a part of all this, I was kneeled over her with my hand gripped on the mask. All I was able to see was a dry, but still smooth chin before I jumped back, surprised, after hearing Mom's voice.

"Alex," was all that Mom said. It was all that she could say.

It was a relief to see that she wasn't dead, but when I left the Rebel and crawled over to Mom, my relief ended.

"Mom, don't speak," I begged. Beginning to look around, I assured her that I was going to get help. I tried to comfort her by saying this though I had no idea how completing a task was remotely possible. Lifting the gun from Willie as Mom busted through the door, the Rebel fired. I could see there in front of me the reality I tried to avoid. While I'm sure there was a crack coming from the door hitting against the wall, the crack heard came from the gun responsible for leaving Mom there with a steady stream falling from the gap there on the left side of her body.

"Hush and listen, Alex, dear," she whimpered. I could see that every word said and breath exhaled brought with them pains she cricked and flinched from, but still, even though forced, she remained softly smiling.

I remember there being a silence as if everything surrounding us, too, held its breath. For a brief moment, no more shots echoed towards the distance; sirens seemed to finally take an intermission. It seemed as though the sun I remember hearing laughing, too, wanted to hear what the last words of Mom would be.

Finding a way to ignore the obvious pain, "Alex, please take care of Willie. I've done all th-that I can. You are strong enough to endure whatever it is that's still to come. You've already dealt with more than most people will have to deal with their entire lives and now, it's finally time to show the world the results of this. We're proud of you, dear. I am, your father is, and so is Ms. Darlene. We will all be looking over you, dear."

Looking directly in my eyes, she then said, "You are beyond capable." Her eyes, though looking at me, began looking past, through me. Hollowness became tangible. Intermission ended.

I didn't care who it was running down the hill of Milligan. Though they were too far to confirm whether it was a person running from fear or a Rebel searching for their next victim, I had enough time and used every bit given to drag Willie's fainted body into the house. Finally and suddenly, the songs of the sirens, screams of sorrow heard by people probably enduring the same tragedy I was right then, and similar sounding cracks began again and continued throughout the night. Before shutting the door, I was able to take one last look at Mom. It was the last time I would see her.

"I love you, too, Mom," I said before I slowly and silently shut the door as a screaming man ran past the house and up the street.

In the morning, though scared senseless, I peeked through the window blinds and saw neither the bodies of Mom nor the Rebel. While neither of the bodies were there, the stains of both of their final beings remained.

16

That night, and throughout the following passing days, I surprised myself. For the first time, I found myself engaged in the commitment and purpose of life I declared years before. Long before losing Ms. Darlene and Mom, I decided I would raise and provide what I could for Willie. This was no longer simply declared but was now in effect. Though nothing more than a sibling, I was ready for the responsibility supposedly upheld by a parent.

Are you ready?

Regardless of whether or not I was, I had to act as if I was and had long been prepared for the task at hand. There was no longer a cushion present to comfortably fall on if I made a mistake. A mistake made now would be falling face first on concrete—from a skyscraper.

Now, I had to become the epitome of *Strength*. I thought about and tried to accept this all night.

Hours later, finally waking up from fainting outside, "Where's Momma, Alex?" Willie asked that night.

I struggled to even look him in the eyes when he first asked this. Whether it was because of age or the soft personality he naturally had, in comparison to me, he was a lot closer to Mom than I was. That night, I was blessed that Willie could read the grief that was worn on my face.

Asking one last time but only to be responded to by my silence and continuous refusal to look him square in his eyes, finally, he said in a quiet confirmation, "She's gone, Alex." Hearing him say this was weird. As he began to cry in my arms, without knowing it, he confirmed this for the both of us. So easily and quickly he confirmed what I immediately struggled to accept despite first-hand witnessing it.

Beginning from the very moment I snatched Willie from the yard, pulled him into the house, and shut the door while Mom still laid there in the yard watching nothing, I was calm. Thinking back to it now, until Willie woke up and confirmed that Mom was dead, I was shockingly calm. Not a single tear fell from my face. Not a trace of fear breached my mind. Nothing broke the spell I put myself in. I *knew* that all that had recently happened was nothing more than a nightmare.

I didn't even try to wake myself up. I forced myself to believe that it was all temporary. I told myself that at any moment, like the many mornings before, Willie would snatch me from my sleep with his unapologetic smile showcasing his widely-gapped front teeth. Bent over and in my face until I finally woke up he would take the opportunity to annoyingly remind me that it was yet again time to go out volunteering to clean up another portion of East Knoxville alongside many of the others of the community. Or maybe, I thought as I sat there along the wall thinking in our living room only slightly lit by the single orange-gleaming street light on the other side of the street, maybe, *when* I wake up it would be time to head to school. *When,* not if, I kept reminding myself, *when* there at the school, I would ask Mr. Hodge when would be the next time I could cut his yard.

After hours of searching for a repression that might as well have been hiding from me, all it took was that brief confirmation. "She's gone, Alex," was all I needed to hear to break the spell. Willie saying this revealed to me that I was stagnantly waiting to wake from reality, not a nightmare. Thanks to him, I began accepting what was and would remain.

What took us weeks of effort to rebuild was re-demolished in that single night. Unlike before though, without having to leave the house, based off of what could be seen from just briefly peeking out of the blinds, what I looked at now looked to be a direct part of ground-zero. The immediate time following the beginning of all of this brought with it abrupt modifications. In a community I grew up in, and thus considered myself to being well-acquainted with, I lost any and all the familiarity I once held in the palms of memories.

With the lack of songs heard, it seemed that in response to the flocks of terror, even the birds chose to evacuate from the progressing destruction. More Rebels were being seen running, marching, streaming, searching up and down Jefferson to the point where I decided that it was unsafe to even remain downstairs in the living room of the house. I authorized that Willie was to remain upstairs in Mom's bedroom unless otherwise necessary, though in my head, nothing, absolutely nothing could bring such a necessity.

The few times I had to go downstairs, whether for food or in response to anxiety causing me to question whether or not I locked the front and back door, if never before, those times I creeped down the hall and steps, I felt it was possible that my heart could pound through the bones there in front of it. Especially when I went down the steps, the creaking of the wood seemed to be as loud as an entire orchestra. Though I told myself that the thought was absurd, I stayed falling victim to the fear telling me that if outside, surely any Rebel could hear and if so, that was it.

Failure.

Days continued to pass. Being built by the bulks, more confusion on what to do was being felt. Constantly hearing and remembering Mr. Hodge's "People don't care until it's at their front door" statement, I realized that by this point, his statement had become irritably null. The "*it*" he spoke of was no longer at the front door. The "*it*" he spoke of had by this point walked through the front door and had become fully comfortable. As possible as it was that, by now, it was far too late, I finally realized the importance of knowing.

I found myself desperately interested in knowing who these Rebels were. What did they want? Why did they find it necessary to murder Mom? Though I hated to read, I found it necessary to turn on the news, but to mute it with subtitles turned on. This though provided no new or valuable information. The same things were stuck on repeat. The news provided no new information other than what was already known, or in my case, not known. I wondered if nothing new was being shown because the show wasn't being broadcasted live. Anyone would be stupid to be at the station during all of this. That's if they were still alive to be stupid.

"No, duh, this is a state of emergency. It's common sense that it is safer to stay inside," I found myself saying out loud a few times after the alert was repeated. The more I watched the news the angrier, more scared I became.

It got to the point where signifying which day of the week each sunrise and sunset proclaimed it to be became an insignificant bit of information. The uniqueness of the separate days no longer existed. The looking forward to the weekend on a Tuesday morning was a desire completely extinguished. The satisfaction of making it to a Friday evening, even if it was a short week, lay shattered. The irritation felt when Sunday night finally came and that meant a full five days of school was now a desired blessing that I felt would never again be found. The only difference between the passing days was that the following day brought with it a further addition to the fear established by the previous day.

"Alex, I'm hungry," I heard Willie mumble just sitting there at the front of the bed. I didn't respond as if choosing not to do so would cause his hunger to go away.

Our food supply alone was a battle I wasn't sure how we were going to overcome. I took notice of this the very first day all of this began; I could tell that our food was not going to last long. Mom had intended to go to the grocery store. She was a cash only type of person.

Because she told me a million times, it was easy to remember her telling me that if you have a certain amount of money in dollar bills, able to be seen, it's that much harder to place yourself in financial problems. In her pocketbook upstairs, I saw the 120 dollars she planned to go to the grocery store with, but at this point what would that have done? It didn't take going to the store to know that the value of money instantly and completely became worthless. Even if I decided to go sneak to a grocery store, getting all the way there *and* back was yet a whole different problem. Never before had living in what Mr. Hodge told us was considered a "food desert" seemed like such a significant curse.

Not only did we not have much to begin with, but going to get some was even more dangerous. The news showed several videos of stores being ransacked and others burned. Though the TV was muted, watching as the news showed a convenience store being demolished, one of the videos replayed the most had a Rebel so close to the camera that was recording. As the eyes remained looking at the camera, almost seeming to be looking and taking notice of where we were, though a mouth could not be seen moving, the simple black and white subtitles read, "This is last America! This is last Ameri—"

"Alex, I'm *hungry*," Willie again said, but this time a little louder to ensure to both of us that if I didn't reply there was no denying that I heard him.

"You are more than old enough to go fix something to eat," I yelled reflexively.

He simply sat there on the other side of the bed looking down towards his crossed legs. Though this wasn't the first time, several times Willie relied on me to provide food. Every single time he did this, I wondered whether it was a curse or a blessing in growing up in a single parent household. Many times I thought it was a curse. A number of times at school, especially after seasonal breaks, friends would talk about the dinners their mothers *and* fathers were able to make. *Together.* They would talk about great dinners they were able to enjoy without stress. For us, though, not constrained just to seasonal dinners, as much as she desired to provide, Mom was unable to dedicate the time it would take to make such dinners. Stubbornly, but still with desire to show me and Willie the necessity of having a good work ethic, even when Ms. Darlene told Mom that she didn't need three jobs, Mom maintained each of them. Though there were a few times Mom found a way to still provide awesome dinners, this was not often. Simple dinners were a constant presence.

Still, especially now, I saw the possibility of Mom not being able to teach us how to cook as a blessing. Because she couldn't teach us, and because Ms. Darlene was too brittle to barely be able to stand up for an entire 10 minutes, let alone to cook or clean, every other "domestic duty" had not been learned. So I taught myself. What if there were other kids who recently lost their parents? Once gone, what then of those kids—even if they were my age? Were they capable of lasting one full day due to their level of dependency on their parents? Maybe a forged perception, maybe not, but never before had the sacrificial absence of a hard working mom seemed such a blessing.

Regardless of if I chose to see the situation we were in as a curse or blessing, one thing was for certain: I was stupid because instead of teaching Willie the few things I was able to teach myself, over the years, I simply provided for him and thus created the same cursing dependency I saw in the kids and teens of those *great* nuclear families. It was equally my fault that at a time like this, his survival depended heavily on me. Despite my striving to uphold my vow to be there for him, it was impossible to deny that Willie's dependency was taking an immediate toll on my patience with him. During this time, where riots were literally knocking at our front door, there I was cooking Mac n' Cheese for a soon to be 11 year old.

Still sitting there on the bed having not said a word for several of the past minutes, I submitted and carefully walked downstairs to make him—us—something to eat.

Out of nowhere, crumbling a silence that seemed natural, "Alex, they're coming again!" Willie managed to both shout and whisper.

He saved our lives at the cost of his. It was a day that I knew I would never forget. Down Milligan and up Jefferson, cohesively they could be seen stomping, in unison, together as a herd. White and black dressed, colorless-stripped American flagged-masked Rebels came trooping up the streets knocking out windows and setting remaining cars in driveways on fire. They marched, silencing spontaneous screams I'm sure could be heard far down the other side of Cherry Street. As they marched, I saw that some broke from the collective-ness and went into homes to kill the few they must have caught peeking through the other side of window blinds.

This past day, curiosity *almost* killed the cat. I remember it being somewhere around 6:30 in the evening. You could still hear the short spurts of panic happening from neighboring blocks, but quickly, the closer they got to passing our house, the easier it was to hear the sound of their steady metronome march growing. Our lights were cut. Though it was already muted, I ran up the steps to completely cut off the TV. Blinds were shut. In almost a single jump back downstairs to be there with Willie, the closeness of their march signified that it was now too late to yank him back upstairs and risk the creaking of the steps revealing our presence. Nowhere else to run, Willie now in my arms, I found ourselves scrunched into the kitchen's closet. Our silence combatted with the sound of their march. I could now tell that they were crossing in front of our house.

There was just enough space for both of us to fit, but barely enough space for us to sweat. I seemed to taste the wood of the shelves every time that I took a breath.

Out of nowhere, "Our F-Father..." Willie began to sob as I heard his hands clap together. When he prayed, he always closed his eyes excessively tight but I still knew, at this time, though his eyes here tightly closed they were not as tight as he wanted them to be.

"...which art in h-heaven h-hallowed be thy name..."

"Shut the hell up!"

The irony, I thought with a brief grin.

"...on Earth as it is in Heaven. Give us this day, our daily bread, forgive those who trespass as we forgive our trespassers ..."

Their march remained passing. It was mesmerizing. As my pulse and heartbeat began synchronizing with their beat, sweat, too,—in crowds—began to dance, slipping smoothly down our bodies.

"...the power and the glory forever, amen."

It didn't take long, and the march slowly faded, but we stayed put choosing to endure the heat of that small closet for at least another 20 or so minutes. Finally, I figured it was safe to leave the kitchen.

"Stay here for just a second," I told Willie while slowly opening the closet. Though every light of the house was off, when the natural light came through the door and down to Willie, I could barely tell the streaks of sweat from the tears I knew he had released. Risen up to examine our safety, I could see, before leaving him, that despite the constant whimpering of his face, Willie struggled to show me compliance before closing the door.

Creeping out of the closet, heart bumping along with the landing of even the softest sounds of the single steps taken, there before reaching the window in the living room, I stood, paused completely. In a final attempt at repressing everything, I locked my eyes shut hoping, almost praying that when I opened them, it would all be gone; I wished this would not even be a nightmare, but one of those times that Mr. Hodge went on ranting and I left the classroom in a daydream. I wished I'd snap back after hearing the school bell ring for our dismissal. I was hoping that when eyes opened, it would now be time that I had to walk down MLK Jr. Avenue and I would look for and locate Willie still there hanging in his school's courtyard.

Blessed to see that all of what was recently experienced—the deaths, the nightmares, the destruction—was nothing more than a daydream of things I feared would happen, I would take the opportunity to skip hopping on the bus with Willie and rhetorically ask if he wanted to instead walk with me. Regardless of his answer, we would walk together up a few streets and then down Magnolia Ave., past a now abandoned KFC, past what used to be a Walgreens, and all the way down, finally passing one of Knoxville's most popular McDonald's. While walking, at some point, we would eventually be passed by busloads of both of our classmates.

I wished for this. Eyes still closed, I prayed for this, but when I opened my eyes, nothing changed. If it could be counted as a change, the only thing that did change was that when my eyes opened, instead of standing there stuck with that small essence of empty hope present, I was curled on the ground, bawling. Realizing how loud I was, fear sprang through my body and forced me to cease. Finally able to regain my composure, after getting up and walking over to separate the blinds and see what was now on the other side of the window, for the second in a short period of time, paralysis.

As if already anticipating, I looked through the blinds and there in a straining stillness was the mask, were the eyes looking directly at me. On the other side of our blinds was the solemn mask belonging to existences sure to be historically associated with the providers of a fear outmatching "the fear of God."

There stood a Rebel with thick, short black hair barely visible under the edges of the mask. In silence, his tilted head was only inches away from the same window that was only inches away from me. Within what was no more than a second, an infinite eternity had crept between us. I couldn't scream. Not because I didn't want to scare Willie. I couldn't scream because I was frozen by a contradicting heat felt when my stricken eyes took notice of the Rebel's dark brown eyes.

"This is last America," the Rebel shrieked loudly as if announcing this to an audience of a thousand listeners. The Rebel then pulled his arm back and ferociously, with his bare hand, punched against window. With every punch, the window cracked more until the Rebel's hand came straight through the window.

Violent pushes through the broken window now in pieces on the floor allowed the window curtain and blinds to be vigorously ripped and laid out over crumbles of sparkling glass. The all-white clothing of the Rebel's attire reached a point where it could've been considered tie-died. In spots all over, a full-red was now layered across his mask and his clothing was becoming more tainted as his gushing hand continued to surge against the remaining shards of glass still attached to the borders of the window's frame.

Like a prideful warrior standing on a hill after a battle, silhouetted by the setting sun behind him, the Rebel stood there before taking the first step through what was left of the window.

"No!"

I clearly heard this and initially thought it came from the Rebel speaking to me as I was already tripped up and crawling backwards.

The second that I saw the Rebel beginning to crawl through the window, the constriction of fear snapped there and then. The freeze holding me melted. Before I could even begin to understand, I had started to frantically scramble and drag myself back towards the kitchen. But the voice I heard wasn't the Rebel's. Out of nowhere, I felt—what in a short period of time had become so familiar—that same crack that brought with it a quick stab against my eardrums. It was a crack identical to the one I still remember hearing before Mom was hollowed-out.

"Alex, come here," breathed Mr. Hodge standing there bent over with hands rested on his knees, there on the other side of what used to be the living room's window. "Rebels are on their way back here. Listen closely. In my house there are supplies of instant noo—"

I can't help it. Again, like times before back in his class sophomore year, it happened. It was like we were back in his class. Falling away, no matter how hard I tried, I couldn't hear what was being said by Mr. Hodge. Not sure when, but not listening to him at some point became habitual.

Not that it ever took much effort, but as he spoke in portions, in between deep breaths, muting him out was even easier than usual. Unlike ever before, with nothing to prevent the grasp, what I was seeing outside was what fully snatched my attention. The sun, having further set, was still there just above the roofs of houses behind where Mr. Hodge was standing. There was an esthetic orange tint stretched along the sky. *Amazing.* I found a way to notice its beauty while there around us, in the yards of neighbors, dried-blood from where bodies once lay were like newfound decorations purposely placed in certain stations of the individual yards. It looked almost like there was a competition. Who had the best stain-placement decoration? Who was most creative with their placement?

It was easy to notice neighboring houses and then those on the other sides of hills that remained on fire. I wondered then if this was similar to the view Ms. Darlene told me that she remembered seeing that evening her house crumbled from deteriorating flames. Though I couldn't see where the houses' smoke came from, the results of the different houses being on fire were easy to see. Different funnels of smoke from these separate houses raced from their home towards the sky. My feeling and understanding of destruction was no longer intangible. But still, the sky beyond the sprinting smoke remained as a peachy golden-orange veil. Tell me how, at such a time, could the sky remain so soothing to the mind and inviting to the soul? One of the most mocking beauties ever seen.

"Alex!" Mr. Hodge yelled with broadened eyes and hands on my shoulders demanding my attention. "Alex, do you understand?" I was like Willie; my trembles and soft nod answered for me. Mr. Hodge stood there pondering for a second—looked me up and down then turned to stare at the Rebel there motionless on the ground. Yells could be heard and their volumes were increasing. He dragged the body there at the edge of the window, and before pulling the body completely through the yard, Mr. Hodge said with calmness, "Alex, it's all at my house, but be smart about getting it and getting there."

He tossed the body on the side of street. I remembered he took one last back towards me. I'm not sure what was different with Mr. Hodge from when we walked from College Hille. That day, Mr. Hodge continuously stuttered over his words, Fear caused him to jump at even the sound of his own breathing. This day, though, standing there in the middle of the street was again, my first impression of Mr. Hodge. This was the Mr. Hodge that often told me and the class that the strength we had was determined by how we saw ourselves and not by the perceptions of others. As it was back when we were in the school's office, my freshman year, Mr. Hodge stood there, chest *still* lifted. He then trooped off towards the yells that seemed to be only a block or two from us.

Shortly after seeing him sprint back down Jefferson and up Milligan until no longer in sight, I was able to finally go back to Willie.

The sounds of five simultaneous cracks resonating from streets over suddenly beat against, through and then away from my ears until no longer heard. That was the last time I saw Mr. Hodge.

Opening the kitchen closet, Willie was on the ground sleeping, snoring even, consumed in a peace that I didn't know could be reached at a time like this; after all that had just happened was said and done, he slept. Without any energy to do anything more, instead of trying to pull him up, I just knelt beside him wishing to join his peace, the same peace that I craved.

"Alex! What should we do?" Willie stood stiffened with a fear-struck expression, pulling me back from remembering all that happened no more than two or so days ago.

It was the same approaching metronomic march. Remembering the sacrifice, the beauty of the day, and the peace that both of us found ourselves able to somehow manage to reach, I just smiled. Remembering how he was and how he would remain oblivious to near everything that happened days before, I whispered to him, "Same as we did before. Go to the kitchen closet." And for the rest of the night we stayed there, listening as the metronome march passed by.

17

"What's wrong Alex?" Willie asked me earlier this day. For days now, our house might as well have been just as vacant as one of the empty neighboring houses. Electricity remained turned off. To keep track of its arrival, the TV was briefly turned on at night to the news channel—still muted—to tell me how far away the special day was. Though it was on and off in a matter of the two or so seconds it took me to locate the date, despite the lack of intention to pay attention to anything more, a headline was able to be read within a twitch of my eyes.

"America, death tolls are rising by the hundreds with every one of the individual attacks. We are at war." I turned the TV off.

"What's Wrong, Alex?"

I said nothing but thought loudly, *Gee, Willie, I don't know. It's nothing to obvious. I've felt like I've had the flu for the past few days, the death toll is declared to be rising, the sound of metronomes continue to pass by what seems like every other hour throughout the day and night, and our food has depleted to what seems like one stale chip for each meal of the day, but other than that, everything is just peachy, Willie. Peachy*

I thought all of this, but what caught me off guard was a thought that came when I turned the TV off and heard, outside, their march marching through the streets.

You. Willie. Willie, you're what's wrong.

18

September 15th had come. "Happy birthday," I said with a forced smile. How in the world could it be happy though? There was now *no* food, barely any crumbs for even the rats and roaches to eat in our house. Knoxville seemed to be fully incarcerated by an incomprehensible silence. Other than us two, it sounded like Knoxville had been fully emigrated and abandoned; that or near everyone within the city wasn't as fortunate as we were.

Or were they the fortunate ones?

Shriveling fires showcased the trademarks of the Rebels. I'm sure Willie sensed my sham and so forged a smile to match mine.

Since the few days before, I had one thought, one question on my mind. "What's wrong, Alex?" was what Willie had asked. He asked me, but I could've just as easily ask him the same. On his birthday, that Willie I was looking at was not the Willie I had known my whole life. I knew the weakest boy in the neighborhood. Willie, almost known by all as "*the* chicken," but was still the one that had the biggest heart; the boy who had a smile that had the potential to one day outshine the stars of a freakin' galaxy! I always knew a Willie that you had to try to be pissed at despite him often being annoying. I knew a little brother I depended on for my own personal growth.

We were both young, but far more experienced than most. Whether he knew it or not, I depended on him because he was my teacher. We always saw and handled the same things so differently. Since I can remember, I've felt we've always had something to prove. By 10, I comprehended that there were social expectations. Being of the lower-class in an upper-class environment set aside as a part of a still mainly lower-class portion of Knoxville, people still expected us to dress a certain way.

With money she was able to scramble together, Mom had bought Willie some Converse shoes for his birthday last year. Walking home from school, we overheard a kid whisper, "who did they steal those from?" While I was enraged, Willie laughed just as much as the kids around us. Several times, kids and grown-ups would say things that would piss me off, while Willie maintained that same smile as if it was etched onto his face. The smile whose joy could be seen as *the* epitome of the term "joy," was now the same one that had become absent.

"What's wrong?" he asked. It was the same question that I wanted to ask him. At least I wasn't a typically happy person, but him, things changed when the frown not only came but remained. Of all that happened over the course of days, this was one of the eeriest.

I was angered after I told him happy birthday. His thank you smile was not *the* smile. At the time I needed it most, Willie alone deprived me of the thing, the second breath I found myself needing more than anything else. Though he alone could give all that I needed, all that he gave me was the same emptiness I had grown used to giving him.

I was even more saddened because, on his birthday, I continued to grow even sicker and more fragile.

"Happy birthday," I had managed to still tell him, but in the same minute, he had already asked if I was hungry.

"Am I hungry?" A quick transition came from being pissed and fragile to enraged, scared.

"We have no food and you need to eat, Alex. You said a few days back that there was food at Mr. Hodge's right? I can run over to get some food. His house isn't that far from here. You're horrible, Alex," Willie continued considerately speaking to me.

"What in the World? These Rebels are all around and you want to go get food?"

"I just want to go—"

"I swear I will break you if you step out that door, Willie," I said barely knowing what word would follow the one before. Right then, I could see that any chance of seeing his beautiful smile ever again left at that moment. His expression replied that he was not scared of me; he instead pitied me.

"Get your rest, Alex," as he began shutting the door

"Willie, I swear—"

The door shut before I could finish. For the short period of time I was able to before almost dying, I held my breath and waited to hear if the door downstairs would open or shut. I listened for even the slightest sound that signified him sneaking out. I listened to hear even the softest creak that would rat out that Willie was going down the steps. I realized that, right then, something was happening I never knew was possible; I feared Willie's selflessness.

He would still go. I could feel it. So I waited. If it meant saving him, though barely able to shift positions in Mom's bed, at that moment, I swear I was ready to break him. I almost get mad thinking about it. What I now see as stupid logic, if it meant saving the life of my loved one, my *last* loved one, ready to use every bit of remaining life left within me to fulfil my self-proclaimed purpose of life, there was nothing I wasn't ready to do, even if it meant in several aspects, breaking him.

I kept dozing off and suddenly waking up. After eyes shot open, I'd yell for him and walking from where I was sure was our room, he would stick his head through and around the opening of door. He would do this and stay there, but each time, he never said a word. I only stared back until he eventually brought the door back until it was almost fully closed. It became a cycle. "Willie!" one time. "Willie!" a second time. "Willie!" a third, fourth, and fifth time. The same, over and over again, he would only peak through without saying anything beyond the pity his face screamed.

"This is last America!" This was the phrase that had already woke me up several times. It, too, was a part of the cycle. "This is last America," woke me several times in a sweat. It was the evening time. Outside, what could be seen through Mom's room's window blinds, it looked like the same evening that had been there a year ago; the evening that was there before any thought and fear of the coming danger was remotely considered.

It was crazy. Regardless of what may or may not be happening, if I simply watched and studied the sky, it did seem to sympathize or correlate with us… humans. Not a single storm had happened since Mom's death or the hundreds of others. There had not even been the rainless thunder storm nights where lightening would streak along the canvas of the completely pitched sky. This whole time, the past days and then some, the sun had just remained—smiling. Of the many, just barely outdoing Willie's selflessness, the savaging sun's caress became one of the most agonizing things.

Feeling guilty for having yet to provide even the slightest bit of compassion on his birthday, I decided to get up to at least hang, even if just a few minutes, with Willie. I walked to our room, but he wasn't in there. I don't remember hearing any creaks from him walking down the steps, but I considered he may have walked down the steps while I was dozed off. Because of the danger, especially because it was evening, the time it would be the easiest for any of the

Rebels to see and get him, I quickly grew mad, but just a quickly threw out the anger with remembering why I got out of bed in the first place—to comfort and be around him.

When I got down the steps and slightly hurried over to where I was sure he would be, I quickly saw that he wasn't sitting down in the kitchen. Considering the possibility that somehow I rushed by him without noticing him, with no fear of being seen through the absented window, I then ran to the living room, but he wasn't there either.

Everything grew silent and became nothing. My heart became conservative and chose to skip in hopes of saving the few of its remaining beats. *He did it,* I heard a whisper say as a heat of rage consumed me and burned every bit of pain no longer felt; it was now gone without a single trace that it even once existed.

Our front door was left barely open, and I was already in the middle of the street before I realized it. Never had the sound of that now familiar resonation, zipping towards the horizon hurt as if what created it was pointed towards me.

I swear I'm not crazy. Looking up and down the street, between two jerks, she was right there and then gone. To this very moment I swear I saw Ms. Darlene pointing from the corner of Jefferson and up along Milligan. When I snapped back to see her again, she wasn't there, but I still ran. On Milligan, bolting past Woodbine, not holding back a single tear leaping down to the blazing streets below, just as it was with Ms. Darlene, in between two blinks, I saw Mom. She was there at the corner of Milligan and East Fifth, body facing me but looking to her right, and after a single blink, she was no longer there.

For a second, I thought I was losing it until I unmistakably heard, "Mr. Hodge's house," from a voice that sounded to be right there running behind me, pushing me. Finally on East Fifth and running to Mr. Hodge's, it suddenly hit me. You told me. Right then, I thought it was instinct, but now, remembering it all, I know for sure that it was You.

When first getting there though, I saw nothing. The lawn mower was in the same exact place I left it when all of this first began. *Go to the backyard*, I thought and then went. I went and saw what would bring to me another full paralysis. Just after cutting the corner of the house, I saw Willie bent over on his knees as if the Rebel was God; as if this Rebel standing before him was the God he was praying to for protection and security when we were in the closet those few days back. Blood was in a stream to the ground from Willie's left arm. I noticed the red-tainted, wrinkled black shirt and crumbled pants of the Rebel. Above was a dirty cloud in front of a sun slowly leaving us to see another show—seeming to be bored with ours.

No. Not this time. Breaking the paralysis, "Willie," was all I remembered screaming before I could comprehend what I was doing. One last time, as I ran, I found myself still waiting for all this to be a dream, but came to the understanding that until I woke, it was a nightmare in full existence. Coming from behind Willie, unable to yet see his face, as he heard me shout his name, his head began rotating. What broke me was not the *one* second I realized separated his living from his death. No, as he turned, he gave me what I had long been needing. Now able to see his face as he turned his head just enough, I saw that Willie was smiling; providing to me *the* beautiful one.

Screw the sun, I heard a thought screech; I agreed. The smile I was seeing had an undiscovered genuineness to it. It was the smile alone assuring to me, "Alex, it's finally over." His smile tried to tell me that there was a beauty in his dying. No more struggle, No more hunger. All the sleeping he could ever want, but thanks to me, it sucks that it was the last time I would see it, as his smile began to shift.

Three cracks individually echoed. Two were close together and then came a final one. I looked down and confirmed to myself that I was shot in the arm and in the stomach, but I felt neither. Still unable to comprehend the pain that I knew was somewhere close by, I was able to see that the Rebel, too, was struck spread out motionless on the grass. The gun was in my hand, and I was laid out frantically trembling on my side.

Willie was right there over me crying. I was fading in and out. All I could see was that Willie was over me screaming, and pulling me up and down, but I only heard a steady ring—that final shellshock.

The last thing I remember was being able to read his lips. My eyes finally closed after reading him call me something I only allowed him to call me and no one else, but still something he rarely called—out of respect. Sadness and anger were the only times he used this. I faded completely out after reading his lips scream it.

"Alexandria."

What a birthday, William.

19

Crack I heard one last time before I woke up here.

You asked me to tell, and that's all that I remember being able to tell. That's the last thing I remember. I've never been a person of regrets, but I wish there was more that could've been done; more that I could've done. If I can ask, is Willie dead, too?

"Yes."

I won't even ask for me. In comparison to them, their hearts, spirits, sacrifices, their selflessness, and then my disbelief in, I guess, You, who am I to claim whether or not I deserve whatever is next. I guess, in case they were unable to ask before dying, God, if even necessary, will You forgive them—Ms. Darlene, Mom, and Willie, any and everything that could possibly keep their lives from being seen as "pure?" I feel as though they deserve the best of whatever is to come next. Especially Willie. I loved him like no other.

You know, it's ironic. It's ironic that now that I think about it, the strength I spent my whole life trying to portray was something that was natural to him as well as Ms. Darlene and Mom. No matter what I did, the strength I was almost willing to sell my life and soul for still wouldn't have amounted to anything in comparison to what I can now see they always had. Now that I've told and remembered it all, so many times, if I wasn't so caught up in trying to raise Willie, who knows what he could've taught me.

If it matters to anything, would you please bless them?
"Yes."
Thank You.
Success.

EPILOGUE:

Alex was one of the millions swiftly affected by the implosive terror attack which started within America. Without recognition, many of the Rebels invading Knoxville were everyday citizens. One of America's worst fears came from Americans. From the very beginning, defenses against these attacks were ineffective. The population of Rebels included soldiers, law enforcement, teachers, professors, husbands, wives, pastors, doctors, and so on to the point where trust became a forgotten part of existence for many.

Fulfilling its purpose, the mask worn by the Rebels concealed true identities until it was too late. By the time many were able, it was too late to ask "How long have they been present?" and "How many are there?"

The implosion grew until it became an international plague clearing out cities and countries by the populations. The existence of the Rebel fear was only temporary. With quickness, as people began fighting back against the Rebels, and sometimes seeing who the individuals behind the masks were, they then also fought their own paranoia. Implosion after implosion. Division after division. One thing that never changed, as time progressed still, the sun remained smiling.

"Wow. You're just as beautiful as I remember."
"Who in the world are you?"
"Ha! Still as tough, too!"
"That smile. Willie! But you look—"
"We have a lot to talk about, Alex."